THE CROWNS' ACCORD

KEEPER OF
DRAGONS

BOOK 4

J.A. Culican

Edited by: Cassidy Taylor

Cover Art by: Christian Bentulan

ISBN-13: 978-1983661761

ISBN-10: 1983661767

www.dragonrealmpress.com

For my eldest daughter, Julianna and her wish to share
bedtime stories of dragons and adventures with all.

Contents

Chapter One

I dove into the lake, slicing through the calm water. The coolness was refreshing, and I swallowed a few big mouthfuls because my throat was dry and raw from all the shouting during combat training.

Coming up for air, I looked across the field to make sure the Mere Blade was still leaning against a nearby rock in its scabbard. The wondrous sword the mermaids had let me use would cut through almost anything just like butter. That included the training swords, so for training, I had to use a normal training blade. We weren't trying to kill anyone, after all.

As I slogged out of the lake, water streaming off of me and dripping from my clothes, I used my hands to wipe as much water as I could out of my hair. My mop had started out shaggy and was now actually getting long. I had decided to let it grow out so I could eventually put it in a ponytail. Eva told me she thought it would look good on me, and I trusted my best friend's judgment.

Dirt and sand clung to my feet as I slid them into my sandals, but they'd dry out soon and be easy to clean. Eva stood on the lakeshore, watching me. She had an amused smirk on her face. "Sometimes I think you're turning into a mermaid. If you spent as much time training as you did swimming, maybe you wouldn't be so clumsy with your sword."

I stuck my tongue out at her. "Haha. Just because you'll only go swimming when Cairo is in the water doesn't mean you enjoy it any less than me. Speaking of Cairo, where is your *Vera Salit?* I saw he and Jericho left halfway through the morning session, but I didn't see them come back."

Eva looked around as if only noticing for the first time that Cairo was gone. I didn't buy her act. With those eagle eyes of hers, she knew where Cairo was all the time. She replied, "Probably helping the Elves rebuild Paraiso. I'm so glad the Elves are back, and they've been treating us a lot better since we rescued them from Eldrick."

I shuddered, and it wasn't from the cool breeze blowing across my wet skin. I wondered if his name would ever stop having that effect on me. "Thankfully, there hasn't been any sign of him these past few weeks, ever since the battle at the castle in Alaska. I hope we never see him again."

"I hope so, too," she said, handing me a towel. "But none of the scouts have seen Eldrick, or the Dark Elves and Elden, or even the Carnites he recruited. Not even the Realm Two scouts have seen them, and I think that if they were anywhere to be found, Realm Two dragons would be the ones to find them."

I looked up at the sun. There was a large gap in the Congo's jungle canopy around the lake. I looked back at Eva and said, "Maybe our break is about to end. Let's go find Jericho and see what he wants us to do. I know we were supposed to help out with some of the rebuilding today, but you know. And like you said, maybe Cairo is with him."

Eva smiled. Of course, she knew where he was, but I played along and smiled back. "Yes, they change our routine every day, usually so we can do more training. I don't know about you, but I would rather rebuild than beat each other up some more. Those sticks hurt."

I was totally on board with that. I was covered in bruises which I hadn't bothered to use my mahier to heal yet. I headed across the training field and grabbed the Mere Blade on my way. Eva followed. I slung the sword over my shoulder and then Eva and I walked together into Paraiso. The Elven capital had been the most beautiful place I had ever seen, and it would be again, someday.

We went to the treehouse everyone had just sort of agreed would be the headquarters for all the building projects. It wouldn't take long for the Elves to regrow their city, but it wouldn't happen overnight, not when it had been torn up so badly by Eldrick's troops. At least the Elves' magic wards were back up, so we didn't have to worry about any wandering humans anymore, or even about enemies finding the place. Okay, that wasn't really true—I still worried about it, but at least we were in less danger of it now that the wards were up again.

When we got to the HQ, I spotted Jericho and Cairo talking with Gaber, Prince of the Elves. Those two had pretty much hated each other since long before I was born, partly because the dragons had abandoned them once and partly because of the thing between Jericho and Clara.

The war had brought them together, and gone a long way toward healing old wounds. Yay for them. I had new wounds to make up for them.

Eva bolted ahead of me and skidded to a stop near Jericho. She stood by quietly, grinning and waiting for him to finish talking. That gave me a chance to catch up—the last thing I wanted to do was more exercise after that last training session.

As I stepped up next to Eva, I heard Jericho say, "You're absolutely right. He should have made a move by now."

Gaber replied, "I know Eldrick better than anyone, though I hate the fact that he's my brother. If he hasn't made a move by now, and he's laying low so well that even dragons can't find his trail, it means he's planning something big."

Jericho's red eyes flared a little brighter, and puffs of smoke left his nose. I could always tell when he was mad, and so could everyone else.

Eva took advantage of the short pause in their conversation. "Is there anything we can do to help right now?"

I cringed a little because when he was puffing smoke like that, it was best to let him talk to you first. His head whipped toward Eva and he snarled. Eva didn't cringe like I had, but then again, she never looked afraid of anything.

"In Aprella's name, what are you two doing standing around?" Jericho snapped. "We don't have time for this laziness. If you had fought the war as slow as you are moving today, we would all be saluting our new king, Eldrick."

I didn't think he was being fair to her, and before I could stop myself, I blurted, "She's not the one you're mad at." When he looked at me, eyes flaring again, I added, "We aren't lazy, we came to find out what we should be doing. It's time to help rebuild Paraiso, right?"

Jericho's eyes flared brighter for an instant, but I didn't back down. That was new for me because before the war, I was afraid when he was talking to me, much less mad at me. He could still be dangerous, but not to me, I had learned. He wouldn't do anything to harm the Keeper of Dragons.

He interrupted my thoughts, yelling, "Why don't you exercise something other than your mouth, for once? Besides, you trying to help around here does more harm than good, clumsy. Let's see how your stamina training has been doing, instead. Both of you, take a five-mile run through the jungle. Hit the obstacle course!"

My jaw dropped. He was obviously more upset than I had thought. I tried to apologize, but as soon as I open my mouth, he barked, "Do it now!"

Okay, maybe things hadn't changed as much as I had thought because before I had a chance to even think about it, I found myself running through Paraiso toward the jungle. My heart was pounding with something suspiciously like fear.

Eva was only a couple steps behind me as we made our way through the trees lined with their once-gorgeous treehouses, and headed toward the thicker, wild jungle outside of the Elves' capital. Once we burst through the tree line, we had to slow a little bit because the going got harder. It didn't take long to feel hot again, and I soon had little beads of sweat building on my forehead.

We got to the beginning of the obstacle course a few minutes later that marked the start of our five-mile run. The O-Course was a marked path through the jungle that took us across all sorts of terrain. We'd have to jump, duck, vault over things, swim across a big stream, go up and down rocky hills that were more like giant boulders than hills, all while trying not to twist my ankle by catching it in a root or running over the uneven ground. Every time a tree fell, it tore the root ball up and left a hole, and the torn-up root ball slowly broke down and gathered dirt to become a little mound. The jungle was full of these pits and mounds, and if we weren't careful, it was easy to twist an ankle. The day before, I miraculously avoided twisting my ankle, but Eva had to limp back to Paraiso and get healed. It all added up to make the O-course run my least favorite training exercise of all time.

Breathing heavily, I asked Eva, "Why don't we just summon our dragons and fly over all this? We shouldn't even waste our time with the course. We'll never use this training, not when we can fly."

Panting, Eva said, "You remember the time we had to fly all the way to Ochana, right? Remember how wiped out we were after that trip? Stop complaining and start running faster, Cole!" She took off, pulling ahead.

I didn't speed up, though. It wasn't worth limping back to Paraiso.

After a few minutes, even though I was jumping and climbing over obstacles, my mind wandered and I fell into kind of a trance just listening to my own steady breathing like Jericho had taught us. He said it made it easier to run farther, but I still felt just as tired.

I almost ran into Eva as I came around a bend. She stood in the middle of the trail. I stopped and put my hands on my knees while I sucked in as much air as I could. "What... What's up?" I gasped.

She didn't reply, and I noticed she was staring at something with her mouth open.

I turned to see what she was looking at, and then I froze, too. Far ahead of us, the dimly-lit jungle grew darker, but it wasn't the light that did it. The Congo had become black in patches. The farther back I looked, the thicker the patches became. Even the trees were blackened. Around the spot's edges, bright green leaves weren't as bright, like someone had mixed gray into their colors. I stared for half a minute, and even as I watched, I could see the green-gray plants turning grayer.

In a whisper, Eva said, "It's like they've been burned. They're getting burned without any fire, Cole." I could hear a rising uneasiness in her voice.

I understood the feeling. A shiver ran down my spine, and every instinct told me to run away. It broke my heart to see the beautiful jungle blackening right in front of my eyes. The Congo was starting to die all around us. It was happening even faster than we had thought.

I spit into the dirt and cursed Eldrick's name. "Come on, we have to go warn the others."

Chapter Two

Without a word, Eva and I both leaped into the air together, shifting into our dragons. We flew back to Paraiso as fast as we could. I scanned as far as I could feel with my mahier. In every black area, I couldn't feel anything with my senses. Actually, it wasn't that I didn't feel anything; it was more like I could actually feel the nothing, as if it was something all by itself—something dark and evil. I sensed the jungle's black splotches getting thicker and thicker the farther away I checked, until they grew together into one giant, growing black mass miles away.

When we reached the Elven homeland, Paraiso, we dove. Elves scattered at our sudden appearance. Right before hitting the ground, we shifted into our human forms and landed. As soon as we got our footing, we bolted toward the reconstruction HQ. I figured Jericho would be there since he was putting so much time into helping the Elves. Eva was hot on my tail. When we got close enough to recognize the people standing around the dozens of boards they used to pin up plans and diagrams I didn't understand, I spotted him.

He saw me running toward him and cocked his head, confused. I skidded to a halt right in front of him, panting and ignoring the cloud of dust I kicked up at him.

Jericho put his hand on his sword hilt and looked all around. "What's wrong? Did you see a Carnite?" I could hear the tension in his voice and wondered if there had been sightings, but that wasn't why we were there.

Eva came to a stop next to me, panting as hard as I was. She shook her head. "No. Worse. The black spots we saw on the way to Ochana after the battle for the Alaskan castle. The spots are here. They're in the Congo!"

Jericho's eyes went wide. I wasn't used to seeing fear on his face. He turned to another dragon and shouted, "Go find Prince Gaber and tell him to set up an emergency meeting. Tell them to bring the

Troll king, too. Why are you standing there staring at me? Run!"

He turned to face Eva and me. "Come with me. This is urgent."

No kidding. That's why Eva and I had rushed back so fast. I didn't argue, though, and we followed him as he stormed across the field. He went so fast, I almost had to run to keep up as he left the training area, heading to the Elven meeting hall. His long legs were a blur. I ended up jogging to keep up, and we quickly arrived at the meeting hall.

Prince Gaber was also just arriving, and I noticed he had his weapons on him. He brushed his hands together to knock off the dirt caked on them from reconstruction, then wiped his hands on his trousers. I couldn't tell whether he looked irritated or concerned. I figured both were good reactions, though. "What's going on?" he asked. "Your soldier told me to rush, as though I answer to a mere dragon soldier's summons. I sent a messenger to alert King Evander, just like you asked. He should be here soon."

Jericho put his hands on my shoulder and replied, "Cole and Eva saw something. We'll get into it when Evander arrives. I wasn't trying to summon you, fool, I meant to warn you."

Gaber said, "It isn't healthy to warn me about anything, not here in my own homeland." He scrambled up the tree toward the meeting hall, and Eva and I followed him.

Inside, Gaber took his seat at the head of the table and stared at Jericho as he came in. I took a seat on one side, and Eva sat across from me, but Jericho didn't sit. He paced back and forth, talking to himself and moving his hands like he was having a conversation. I wasn't sure if he really was just talking to himself or if he was letting Ochana know what was going on. I didn't interrupt him since he seemed a little crazy.

The door burst open again and King Evander stormed inside. He looked as dirty as Gaber, and I decided they must have both been working on repairs. He yanked back the chair at the foot of the table, hard enough that it almost flew across the room. He slammed it down on the ground after snatching it in mid-flight, then sat and yelled, "What is the meaning of this? What's the emergency that you feel fit to *summon* me to discuss?"

Well, I thought to myself, at least he was taking it seriously.

Jericho sat between me and Gaber, but he didn't stop fidgeting and shifting in his seat. He said, "The Keeper of Dragons were out training on an endurance run through the obstacle course—"

Evander cut him off, saying, "That's not why you called me here. Tell me what's going on!"

Gently, Gaber said, "Evander, my friend. How many Trolls did you lose to Eldrick?"

Evander looked around the table, then back at Gaber. "A lot. Unless you found a way to make more Trolls today, I'm guessing that's not why I'm here."

I almost rolled my eyes at his outburst, but I caught myself in time. I said, "No, not a lot—*too many*. That's the right answer. We know there are spots dying all over the world because of what Eldrick did to your Trolls, and I'm sorry for that, and not just because there's not enough Trolls left to keep the land healthy."

Eva stood and planted her hands on the table with a loud bang, then shouted, "That's a problem, but we have a bigger problem right here and now. *The Congo is dying.* Whatever those black lands are, it's grown all the way to the Congo, and it's almost here."

Evander's jaw dropped and his nostrils flared. "I couldn't have imagined it had extended this far so quickly."

Gaber nodded. None of us had thought it would, not yet. He said, "Dragon and Elven scouts all say the same thing—the land is mutating. It's like some sort of disease, and it's spreading through the Earth. We've examined some of it, and it isn't just dead. It looks and feels as though it has been burned, but there is no heat. We dug down and saw that the blackened areas go all the way down into the roots."

"It goes deeper than that," Jericho said. "We dug down, too, following the roots to see where it would end. It didn't end. The roots ended, but reports say that it looks like thin, black tendrils keep going, shooting from the root tips. They tried to follow them to see how far they go, and gave up after twenty or so yards."

It was my turn for my eyes to go as wide as saucers. I had no idea it was so bad. "We have to find a way to stop it before it destroys everything! Maybe we can use tilium, if all the Elves and Trolls got together and—"

Jericho cut me off. "The issue is that there aren't enough Trolls left to heal the land, much less sustain it. Tilium won't do it, so to save the Earth, we have to find another way to bring the land back to life. We must do it before it perishes permanently."

"Are we sure it will even die permanently?" Gaber asked. "Do we know that it won't heal itself or learn to fight off the disease?"

Jericho frowned. "It looks dead to me. Dead, but not dead."

I liked Gaber's idea, but we couldn't count on ideas. "This isn't some normal disease. It isn't because of magic. It's because of a *lack* of magic, so I don't think waiting around is how we fix it. I didn't know the Earth could die permanently, though. Do we know how long it takes for that to happen, once it turns black?"

Everyone shook their heads and my heart sank. I had hoped that Gaber, at least, would've been around long enough to know. I could only guess it had never happened before.

"Why don't we reach out to Ochana for help?" I suggested. "Tilium may not be the answer, but mahier could be."

Gaber glowered at me, catching me by surprise. He said, "Dragons aren't the answer. Besides, I don't trust them. The Elden were Elves, once, and this is an Elf problem. We'll work it out amongst ourselves. As the new saying goes, only a fool trusts a dragon to help when it matters."

After everything we'd been through together, I couldn't believe what I was hearing. What would it take for dragons to regain their trust? The Elves were as stubborn as dragons. My heart beat faster and I had to stop myself from doing something stupid. Instead, I shouted, "The whole world is at risk, and the Elves want to hide it and try to deal with it yourselves? If you could have fixed this, you already would have. This isn't the time for stupid grudges."

Gaber's eyes were almost glowing with anger. He clapped his hands twice, and two Elven soldiers grabbed me by either arm. I tried to argue with Gaber but he ignored me as the two dragged me away.

Chapter Three

When I hit the ground, I staggered and fell. I got to my feet and pressed the leaves and dirt off. I might have even spit on the ground, I was so angry. I didn't know what to do, so I decided to head toward the training ground and let off some steam beating up training dummies with wooden swords. I would've liked to cut them into little pieces with the Mere Blade, but even as mad as I was, I knew that might cause some problems. On my way there, I passed a couple of Elves who smiled and waved, but I only glared at them and kept walking. They gave me a wide berth.

When I got to the training area, I picked up a dull wooden sword and sprinted at the nearest training dummy. I aimed at its neck as I went by, and amazingly, I hit right where I was aiming. The *thwack* was satisfying. One step beyond the dummy, I used my momentum to spin around and from behind, I smacked the sword against the side of its head. *Thwack.* I must've hit it twenty more times—*thwack, thwack, thwack*—before I settled down.

If I was being honest, the truth was that it wasn't as satisfying as I'd thought it would be. Once I realized that, the anger came back like a tidal wave. I screamed, my face turning red, and threw the sword as hard as I could. It flew through the air, end over end, in a graceful arc. The metal bands around the wooden hilt glinted in the sunlight right before it splashed into the lake some twenty feet from shore.

I let out another roar. I'd have to go get it. Nothing was going my way. I kind of felt like the sword had it out for me. The Elves had made it, and I felt a little like they had it out for me, too. They were in it together, the Elves and the stupid wooden sword.

I knew that wasn't rational, but as angry as I was, I couldn't help feeling that way.

I wasn't ready yet to go fish the sword out of the lake. Somehow, leaving it in there for a little while felt good, like I was standing up for myself somehow.

I clenched my fists as tightly as I could by my sides and stood looking at the ground as I fought to get my anger under control. I knew I wasn't helping anyone, as mad as I was, and they hadn't really done anything to deserve it. I was just overloaded. Yelling at the Elves might have been satisfying, but it wouldn't get me what I wanted, which was for them to take this seriously and take the help Ochana offered, and work with dragons to try to help save the world. Their stupid pride was in the way.

I really wanted to just punch Gaber in his smug face, but that *really* wouldn't have helped anything. Besides, when I wasn't steaming mad, I liked him a lot and thought the feeling was mutual. He flew off the handle because he's mad, scared even.

Maybe what made me the maddest was just feeling so helpless. I couldn't get the Elves and dragons to work together, I couldn't save the world from black spots I didn't understand and couldn't prevent, and I didn't have any control over my life because I was supposedly this mythical Keeper of Dragons. As if I had asked for that. My whole life, all the way down to that stupid sword landing in the lake, was just out of my control.

With so much anger and nothing to do with it, I actually started to feel like crying. I didn't think I'd ever cried from being angry before, but I could feel my eyes welling up.

I heard the sound of rocks scuffing behind me. Whoever it was, I didn't want to talk to them. I stood still, fists at my side, staring at the ground and hoping they would go away.

Then came a light touch on my arm, and a soft voice behind me said, "Cole, are you okay?"

I recognized Eva's voice. As upset as I was, I knew Eva had nothing to do with it. I took a deep breath and tried not to take it out on her. "No, I don't think I am."

She walked around to stand in front of me, and I could see how concerned she looked. In fact, she looked kind of scared. I hadn't meant to scare her, and it made me feel bad.

I closed my eyes for a couple of seconds, then opened them to look her in the eyes. I said, "I'm sorry, and this isn't your fault. I'm far from okay, but I'm not mad at you."

She clasped her hands behind her back and bit her lower lip, looking at me hesitantly. "You know, whatever is on your mind, you can trust me just like you always have. You're my best friend, and I'd like to think you can talk to me about anything."

I felt some of the anger draining away. It was hard to stay mad with her standing there looking at me. I let out a huff through my nose. "Well, for starters, they threw me out of the meeting."

She looked down and said, "I know. You lost your temper in there. You know most of the Elves don't have a lot of love for the dragons, and you're a dragon. You did talk to him kind of sideways in front of everyone important. Just chalk it up to his pride, and imagine how you would have felt if someone called you an idiot in front of the Ochana council and your parents."

She had a point. I tried not to let that irritate me even more. "That's only part of it. Sure, I got a little hot under the collar, and I shouldn't have. But getting kicked out of the meeting isn't what really got me burning."

She gave me a slight smile and said, "That's what you just said it was."

I clenched my jaw. Clearly, she wasn't going to let me get away with anything, although she was being pretty nice about it. But she only had half the story. "Eva, the only way we're going to win this war is if we all work together. Elves, Mermaids, Trolls, Fairies... And dragons. We're trying, but it's like beating our heads against a brick wall. Everyone seems like they don't trust anyone else, especially not dragons."

She pinched the bridge of her nose, then spread her thumb and index finger out across her closed eyelids. "It's not like the dragons didn't earn it. Maybe you and I didn't have anything to do with it, but we're still dragons. They know that if push came to shove, we would back Ochana. I know your dad has the right idea, and he always pushed the old king to do what was right, but the fact is that the dragons didn't do the right thing. All these other races suffered because of it. How many decades, or even centuries, do you think they had to fight against the Elden and the other evil races with no help from the dragons? Dragons who, I might add, had a sworn treaty to defend them."

I realized what she was doing and gave her a faint smile. "Now you're just playing devil's advocate. You can't really believe there's any reason for them not to trust us now. It's all just about their pride. I'm scared that it's going to get us all killed."

Eva grabbed my hand and gently pulled me toward the shoreline. When we reached a couple of midsize rocks, she sat on one and motioned to the other. I lowered myself down beside her, and she turned to face the water. For a while, we both just sat there together, staring out over the lake. It really was one of the most beautiful places I'd ever seen. I felt more at home than I ever had in Ochana, taking in that breathtaking view. Despite all the Elves.

After a while, she said, "How far do you think the black spots go?"

I thought about it, but I didn't really have an answer. How many Trolls had been killed? Were the black spots growing from every one of those or only some? There were too many questions, still. "I can't give you a solid answer. I can't even really guess. I only know there were a lot of those black dots, maybe one for every Troll Eldrick killed."

She turned her head to look at me as she reached out and put her hand on my forearm. I appreciated the friendly touch.

"Maybe some sightseeing would do you some good. Just fly around and burn off some steam. I know we aren't supposed to be the ones out there scouting, but if we just-so-happened to accidentally fly over the Congo, and accidentally looked at the black area, and then accidentally figured out where it begins..."

At last, I smiled. That was just like Eva. For a moment, my thoughts turned away from our problems as I imagined being up in the sky, flying, free from all this garbage down here. "Well," I said, "I have always been accident-prone. Accidents happen."

She actually giggled at that, which lifted my spirits quite a lot. I smiled back and added, "Besides, wasn't it Jericho who said it's better to ask for forgiveness than permission, sometimes?"

Eva laughed so hard she actually snorted. "Does that sound like Jericho? He didn't say that, and you darn well know it. But it's still good advice. And maybe we'll find a clue on how to fight the blackness while we're out there. Right now, we don't have any ideas."

"Now is a good time to go, while they're up there arguing with each other. If we're lucky, they won't even notice we're gone."

"Who is going and where?" A voice boomed out, and I recognized it as Cairo's.

Startled, I whipped my head toward the sound. I quickly schooled my features, but it was too late. Cairo had heard just enough to be suspicious, I was sure, and my guilty reaction would confirm it for him.

He burst out with a deep laugh, all the way from his belly. That was not the reaction I expected.

Eva and I both spoke at once, tripping over each other. I said we were going to fly over the Congo to let off steam, and she said we were going to go hunt cows in Western Africa. She and I looked at each other, and then we both spoke at once again, this time switching stories. All the while, Cairo kept laughing at us.

"Now, why would you two want to go fly over the Congo?" he asked. "Let me guess. You're hoping to find some clue about the black spots. Am I right?" His eyes still shone with laughter.

Eva was the first to reply. "Fine, you caught us. Yes, that's what we're going to do. Everyone else is too busy insulting each other up there, and nothing is getting done. Cole thinks we need to do something, anything at all, and I agree with him. So, we're going."

Cairo cocked his head. "Oh, so you two are going, no matter what I say?"

I nodded. "You can't really stop us. Maybe you could stop one of us, but then the other would get away and you'd just be sending one of us off alone. That's worse, and I'm sure Jericho wouldn't like it."

Rather than get angry like I expected him to, he grinned again. "Fine, you got me. I was going to try to stop you. But I guess if you're both determined, I can't let you go off alone. That would be totally irresponsible, wouldn't it? I'll just have to come along to make sure you two don't do anything stupid. Again."

I stepped up next to him and put my hand on his shoulder. Suddenly, I felt much better. He was a good man, and I was starting to be grateful he was my best friend's *Vera Salit*. I wasn't sure I believed in it, but I was happy they were getting closer. I knew he'd protect her, no matter what happened. "Thanks, Cairo. Really." I wasn't sure what else to say, but I hoped he understood how deeply I meant it.

He gave me one curt nod, and a look passed between us. I thought, right in that moment, we gained some sort of understanding or connection. I wasn't sure what it was, but I was pretty sure it was important.

He said, "Well, what are you two doing standing around here like a couple of humans? Shouldn't you be up there, accidentally getting into trouble?"

He turned around without another word and jumped, transforming into a dragon in an instant.

With two powerful beats of his wings, he was up and away, streaking skyward.

Eva and I quickly joined him.

Chapter Four

We swept over the treetops, flying low and slow. I soon found the others following me instead of following Cairo. It was kind of weird, being in the lead. When had Cairo switched to viewing me as a leader, instead of a kid who needed babysitting? As I looked down at the black lands below, thoughts about Cairo and that change bubbled in the back of my mind. I wasn't sure how I felt about it.

Everywhere I looked, the jungle had that same burned look to it. From up in the sky, it wasn't as shocking as it had been on foot, looking at the trees directly, but it might've been more horrifying; from up in the air, as far as I could see, the black jungle stretched out to the horizon. Some areas were pitch black, while others were dark shades of gray, giving the Congo jungle a mottled appearance.

Then, about a mile away, I sensed a spot. Since I couldn't sense the black areas at all, I was curious. I looked over and pushed my mahier out to that spot. There was no black there!

In my head, Eva said, "Good catch. Let's go check that out."

Aargh. Again, with the mind-reading. I made a note to ask Jericho how to close my thoughts to casual eavesdropping.

Eva whispered in my head, "Ha, but you'll never block me out. I know you too well. I could probably tell what you're thinking even without you shouting your thoughts all over the place."

I laughed, and a thick trail of black smoke streamed from my mouth. It hit Eva right in the face, which made me laugh even harder. I banked eastward, toward the healthy spot.

We were there in seconds, summoning our humans as we landed. I said, "Look around carefully. Maybe there's something around here keeping the black stuff out. If there is, maybe we can figure out why and make some more of it."

Cairo nodded and began wandering around.

Eva said, "There's nothing here."

I looked around, seeing the whole area for the first time. I had been so focused on finding something interesting that I hadn't really taken in my surroundings. We were in a clearing, and the ground was rocky. Nothing grew on the rocks that covered the spot.

Cairo called out, "Come look at this."

I walked over to where he stood and he pointed at a small clump of grass growing between two rocks. It was black, though.

I spun around and kicked a rock, angry. It went flying into the black jungle surrounding us. "There's nothing here keeping the blackness away. It's just that there was nothing growing here, so we didn't see it. I bet those threads they were talking about are all through the dirt under all these rocks. It's almost like a gravel pit. I wonder what caused it."

Eva put her hand on my arm, reassuringly. "Cole, you didn't think it would be that easy, did you? Trust in yourself. We're going to find something eventually. We just got our hopes up too soon. Let's get back up there and keep looking."

I didn't say anything but simply jumped into the air, summoning my dragon. With a few beats of my wings, I was rising above the tops of the trees. Higher and higher I went, and then I slowly turned back the same way we had been going.

We flew like that for hours, being slow and careful. Everywhere I looked, though, there was the same inky blackness. The farther we went, the darker it got, actually. The dead jungle just went on and on, mile after mile. I figured we had gone far enough to have passed what was on the horizon when we first started the trip, and yet the burned jungle still stretched as far as I could see.

I was getting more and more frustrated, and Eva must have sensed it, because I heard her in my head again. "Cole, there's no possible hope we could ever find the source of this blackness without having to leave the Congo. It just goes too far. If all the other spots have gotten this big, too, we're in trouble."

Yeah, I had figured that out already. I huffed angry smoke from my nostrils and slowly turned back toward Paraiso, hours away to our north. I sent my thoughts out to Eva and Cairo. "Let's get back.

Whatever problems I was having, they're nothing compared to what's going on out here. Thank you both for coming with me. This trip put some things into perspective."

I could feel Eva projecting warm, comforting feelings my way. Cairo replied, "It was my pleasure, Cole. My duty is to keep Eva safe, but the Keeper of Dragons is both of you. We need you in top shape, too. Besides, I thought maybe a dragon's version of taking a long walk might clear your head a bit."

It had. They kept me company, flying on either side as we slowly made our way back north. I still kept my eyes open, just in case we might find something useful, but in my heart, I knew it had been a wasted trip. Not entirely wasted, because I did feel a lot better, I hadn't been lying about that. But we hadn't learned anything useful about the black patches. So, instead of feeling mad enough to punch an Elven prince, I just felt sad and overwhelmed.

Something bright and shiny streaked past my face, interrupting my thoughts and making me pull up short, startled. I hovered, looking around, ignoring Cairo and Eva's questions. Then I saw another bright streak. It shot up from the jungle below, nowhere near us. It arced up and over us, then continued back down to the ground on the other side. There was another, and another. Cairo and Eva saw them, then.

I shouted, "Run!" We beat our wings and streaked away, but I hadn't gotten very far when I felt like I had flown into a web of rubber bands. Hundreds of those bright lights were streaking all around us, then. That's when I noticed they left a thin trail, like a spider web. Where I had flown into the web, they sparkled, becoming visible.

I struggled as hard as I could, fighting to break through, but dozens of the bright flashes were suddenly flying all around me, draping threads over me. They got caught up in my wings. I kept struggling, but I was falling from the sky. Thankfully, we weren't that high. All three of us landed, tangled up, with a painful thump. At least I hadn't broken anything when I landed. I looked at my friends, but they looked okay, too.

I tried to tear away the webbing but couldn't. I snarled, then called for my human. As soon as I transformed, all those threads fell away, hitting the ground and turning invisible again. When I looked up, I could see a sort of shimmer that showed we were basically in a bubble made by thousands of tiny streaking lights. There was no way we could get out of that in our dragon form.

"Run for it!" Cairo shouted.

I didn't have to be told twice. I dug my toes in and took off, running hot on Cairo's heels, Eva right behind me. When we got to the shimmering web shell, Cairo drew his sword and started hacking at it. I couldn't see the threads very well, but it didn't look like he was making any progress. Then I remembered the Mere Blade—I figured it could cut through almost anything, even weird shining webs.

As I reached for my sword, Eva said, "Reach out with your senses. The trap, it's dark tilium." She drew her sword at the same time I did. Dark tilium meant Dark Elves.

I got ready to take a whack at the web shell with the Mere Blade. "As soon as I hit this thing, it's going to cut right through it. Get ready to run."

They nodded and I shifted my grip on the sword hilt. I raised the blade over my head and took a step forward, but then I froze. Just outside the shell, which I could only barely see, there were a dozen Dark Elves charging toward us from the jungle. "Get ready, the Dark Elves are here!"

There was shouting behind me, and I looked over my shoulder. Another dozen Dark Elves were coming at us from the other direction, but they were inside the bubble with us. They must have somehow passed through it. Well, they made it with their tilium, after all. It figured they could get through it. We were surrounded.

Cairo said, "Get back to back. If this has to end here, I'm glad it was with you two. Sorry you had to be here with me, though." He grinned.

I didn't feel like grinning. I felt scared. But I forced a grin on my face anyway. "Me too, friend. If we're going to die, let's take a bunch of them with us."

Eva snarled, "They're going to regret tangling with us before this is over."

I admired her enthusiasm. Just like Eva, always brave, always confident. I wished I could be as brave as she was. Did she even feel fear and was covering it up, or was she just not afraid at all? It didn't really matter, though, because either way, this was a fight we couldn't win. There were just too many of them.

The Dark Elves, twelve in front and twelve behind, stretched out into a circle and then approached more slowly. They had circled us, and the circle was growing tighter.

When they were about 20 feet away, I shouted, "What are you waiting for? Let's get this over with. I promise you're going to regret finding us today." I sounded a lot more confident than I felt.

One of the Dark Elves began to laugh, surprising me. The others joined him. "It was no accident, finding you here!" he shouted back. "But, you silly boy, we aren't here to kill you."

My jaw dropped, and then another Dark Elf said, "But I think by the time Eldrick is done with you, you'll wish we had."

Again, the Dark Elves laughed. It was hard to believe that, just a few months before, those had been Elves. Gaber's people, and probably some I knew. Not anymore.

I reached up with my other hand so I had both hands on the sword's hilt, and adjusted my grip to get ready for them. "I didn't say finding us was an accident, traitor. I just said that it was a mistake. Why don't you come closer, and I'll show you what I mean?"

I spat into the dirt toward them.

The Dark Elves all had swords and shields, and they began to bang their sword blades on the rims of the shields, keeping time. It was spooky, the way the noise echoed through the jungle like an evil heartbeat. And then, altogether as if on cue, they came toward us again. The circle shrank, drawing tighter like a noose around us.

Chapter Five

As the Dark Elf circle drew closer, I thought about summoning my dragon, but there wasn't enough room in the magical web-cage they'd put over us. I wouldn't be able to maneuver, and a dragon stuck on the ground was just a big target. Plus, we had used up some of our mahier flying there, and I hadn't refilled. I wasn't sure I had enough energy left to transform *and* fight, *then* escape. I had to toss the idea.

I heard Cairo shout, "Here they come! Get ready." That snapped me out of my thoughts and back to the situation.

The Dark Elf circle shrank as they got closer to us, and now they stood only a few feet from each other. They stopped banging their weapons on their shields and the rhythmic drumbeat stopped immediately. The effect was kind of scary.

I braced myself, knowing what would come next. For some reason, I really wanted them to just get on with it and attack us, just to get it over with. We couldn't attack them or we'd break up our circle and our backs would be left open. When the Dark Elves stopped just out of our weapons' reach and stood still, staring at us, the whole scene felt creepy.

The one Dark Elf who had spoken before said, "Last chance. You can come quietly. We're supposed to bring you back alive. But, you know, things happen in battle. What's it going to be?"

Eva snarled. "Come and get it, traitors! Fate is on our side. Leave now, and I'll let you live."

I nodded. She had said exactly what I felt.

There was laughter among the Dark Elves. Then he said, "Very well. You had your chance. For Eldrick!" Then the circle surged toward us, all the Elves moving at once to attack us. As they got closer, I saw there were too many of them to get at us all at once. Only about half could fit and still have room to swing their weapons. The other half had to stand back, ready and waiting to fill in any gaps.

The ones in front were inching forward. The instant they got in range, I lunged with my left foot, raised my left arm with an energy field I crafted from my tilium, and thrust with the Mere Blade. Two Dark Elves swung at me, but their blades bounced off my tilium shield. The one I lunged at tried to block with his shield, but my blade point slid through it like it was made of paper.

When I stepped back into a defensive position, I saw blood on my sword and the Dark Elf staggered back, clutching his chest before falling over. He landed on his back and lay still. In a second, one of the Dark Elves from the back row had taken his place, and I was kept busy trying to block their blows. I couldn't find an opening to attack again.

All around me, I heard the *clang, clang* of the battle—weapons hitting shields, swords blocking swords. Twice, I heard someone shout in pain, but neither shout sounded like my friends. I couldn't take time to look, though.

Two of my Dark Elves attacked at the same time, one swinging his sword overhead and the other crouching to swing at my legs. I jumped and drew my knees up, and his blade swept harmlessly beneath me. At the same time, I blocked the overhead blow with my tilium shield, sweeping his weapon aside, and thrust my sword tip downward from above in an arc that caught him in the small area right above where his collar bones came together and kept going. He screamed and fell to one side, tripping up the nearest Dark Elf attacking Eva. That one, too, screamed as she caught him with a wicked diagonal slash of her own. Both our targets hit the ground and didn't move.

My heart leaped for joy when I saw that the three dead Dark Elves were getting in the way of the ones who came to fill the gaps they'd left. That made it hard to reach us, and their attacks were clumsy.

A fourth Dark Elf body joined them, but then Eva shrieked. I had just a second to glance over, and I saw she was bleeding from her left arm. There was another scream from somewhere behind me, one of the Dark Elves attacking Cairo.

The Dark Elves' leader shouted, "Fall back!" The rest stepped away, walking backward until they were out of striking distance.

I took a moment to look around and saw six Dark Elves lying on the ground, and only one of them was moving. He crawled toward his fellow Dark Elves. Cairo let him go, which made me glad. It wasn't that long ago that the Dark Elves had been regular Elves living normal lives, but then Eldrick came along. The fewer we had to kill, the better.

Their leader called out, "You're only delaying this, Keeper. You really think taking out a handful of us is going to save you? There's more where we came from."

I didn't answer, but I didn't like where the conversation was going.

He nodded to another Dark Elf. That one walked away from us about ten paces, then began waving his hands around and talking. I couldn't hear what he was saying, but I felt a strange tickling in the back of my mind. He was casting a spell! I wished I had a bow on me.

As the other Dark Elf kept waving his hands around, the feeling grew stronger. I saw some sort of dark haze rise out of the ground. I tried to look at it with my mahier but still felt that weird sense that the nothing was actually something, all by itself. It was just like with the blackened jungle.

My eyes went wide when I realized the haze was a huge mass of the dark threads we had seen coming off the plant roots. It rose up to form a circle. Then it grew darker and darker. In just a few seconds, it started to look solid, not like mist. The outside edge swirled, like water going down the drain in a whirlpool.

Then the center started to shine. It was a weird, black-and-purple glow, almost like fire embers that cast shadow instead of light. The glowing dot in the center got bigger and kept on growing. When it took up almost the whole once-black circle, leaving just outside edges still spinning, the shadow-glow grew brighter. It looked angry, almost like it was alive.

Suddenly, the whole glowing area disappeared, leaving only the black, spinning outer rim. I could see all the way through the center to the other side. What was on the other side wasn't as it should be, though. When I looked through the hole in the shadow disc, there weren't any trees on the other side, like there should have been. Instead, there was only snow.

Cairo gasped, "What is that thing?"

Then a face appeared in the disk, coming into view from the left just like someone peeking around a corner. Another face appeared on the right. Then, I saw their whole bodies. Dark Elves! First there were only two, but more showed up until I could count at least twenty of them. They lined up in a single-file row, facing me from the other side of the magic disc, wherever that was.

"By Aprella's name, it's a portal," Cairo said.

Eva sounded angry as she said, "Look at all of them. There's got to be two dozen, or even more. I don't think they're standing there just to look at us."

I didn't think so either. They would be coming, and soon. When they got to our side of the portal, I was pretty sure they'd overrun us in a few minutes if not faster, no matter how many we could take out.

From the other side of the portal, someone shouted, "Forward, march!"

Walking in the lock-step, the two rows of Dark Elves started marching forward. They poured through the portal, turning left or right after they came through to make room for the ones behind them. I could see even more Dark Elves getting into line. Dozens more! They kept marching until they had gone all the way around the Dark Elves who were already circling us. They had just drawn the net tight around us, and there was nothing my friends or I could do to stop them.

The Dark Elf leader laughed. "Now what do you think?" he called. "And if you get through them, there's more where they came from. There's always more, Keepers. I'd rather not have to hurt you too much before I hand you over to the king. Just give up, it's hopeless."

Well, it certainly felt hopeless.

Eva shouted, "We've seen what your so-called 'king' does to prisoners. I'll pass. You'll just have to come and get me."

"Very well," the Dark Elf leader said. Then he turned to his army. "I want them alive!" The Dark Elves surged forward, blades and shields ready as they sprinted toward us, leaping over their fallen comrades' bodies to crash into our shields.

After that, the whole scene was just a blur. I dodged, whirled, stabbed, and swung. More Dark Elves fell at my feet, but there were too many. They were going to wear us out just with numbers. Once they realized we were beginning to tire, they got smart, too. They backed off and started toying with us, sending a few at a time to take a swing or two at us before backing out of range, only to be replaced by others. They were wearing us out, while most of them were resting.

Worse, I felt my tillium fading. Every time I blocked some Dark Elf's sword with my shield, it drained me a tiny bit. There were so many attacks coming in, I could feel my battery draining fast. Soon, I'd have to use my tilium, but Eva and Cairo didn't have that. Plus, tilium wasn't as strong as mahier, so I'd lose that even faster than I was losing mahier.

Basically, we were going to lose this fight, no matter how many Dark Elves fell. A glance at the portal showed there were still others lined up on the other side, waiting for their turn to come through.

Eva cried out again and I looked over. She was bleeding from her left leg, just above the knee. She could heal that with her mahier like she had with her arm, but she had to be getting low on power. I could see the pain and desperation on her face, and started to feel something like a black hole in my heart. I was almost ready to just give up and hope they didn't kill us. Or, maybe I hoped they would kill us because I had a pretty good idea of what life was going to be like as Eldrick's prisoner. But if we kept fighting, Eva and Cairo would probably die trying to protect me even after they ran out of mahier. I couldn't let them do it.

I was about to surrender when I heard what sounded like a trumpet off to my right. I couldn't look, though, because I was blocking three Dark Elves as they rushed at me again.

"They're here!" Cairo shouted. "Jericho!"

The Dark Elves didn't pause. If anything, they attacked even harder. I did manage to take one glance over Cairo's head and saw Jericho and Clara standing just outside the dark-magic web shell. My spirits soared until I realized they couldn't get in.

They hacked at the shell with swords, and Jericho breathed fire at it, but it rebuilt itself faster than they could tear it up.

I wasn't sure whether to laugh or cry. With help so close, we were still going to lose. It wasn't fair! Nothing about this was fair. Not me being ripped from my family, not getting plunged into a war I didn't even know on my birthday, and not getting treated like an outcast by many of the other fantastical races just because I was a dragon. I couldn't help what I was.

The black hole inside me, the desperation that made me want to give up, turned warm. Then it got hot. It was filling with fire. Not real fire, but anger. Anger at how unfair it all was. I was enraged—and I was a dragon! Everything around me seemed to fade away as I focused on getting at the Elves attacking us. I became a whirlwind! They were falling in front of me as fast as they could get to me over the growing mound of fallen Dark Elves at my feet.

I saw the looks of fear on their faces as they came toward me, and it made my heart sing. The leader shouted something I couldn't understand, and the

Dark Elf circle backed away from my friends and me. They stopped just outside of that deadly ground in front of me, enough to let us catch our breaths.

Their leader wasn't afraid, though. He looked over to where Jericho and the others were trying to tear down the shell and laughed. "The mighty Jericho! And Clara, it's so good to see you again. You'll never get through the web, fools. You get to watch as we drag your precious Keepers off to your brother, Eldrick. Long live the King!"

"He's no king!" Clara shouted. "He's a traitor, and so are you. Don't lay a hand on them, or—"

"Or what? Your threats are empty. Soon, Paraiso will be empty, too. No Ancestors, no mahier... Only Dark Elves and the one true king."

The funny thing was, the more he talked, the angrier I became. Instead of feeling defeated, I decided that if I was going to get caught or killed, that traitor Elf wouldn't live to see it happen. I summoned all the mahier I still had in me, and my tilium, too. I drew it all into me, into my chest, a growing ball of power. I didn't know what I was going to do with it, but *it* seemed to know. I felt like

I just had to draw it in, and then I could unleash it all at once at the leader and anyone around him. The power knew what to do, even if I didn't.

Suddenly, I felt light-headed. Had I taken in too much power? That was my last thought before I felt everything start to spin. Was I spinning, or everything else? I couldn't tell. My eyes rolled back into my head. A fire-hot wave washed over me, burning me, but I was too dazed to even cry out.

My feet left the ground—I was floating up into the air. There were gasps all around, but I ignored them. Yes... Yes! My power was at the breaking point. I couldn't hold any more of it in, but I still kept drawing it inside me. It was coming to me from Eva and Cairo, too, and then from all the Dark Elves around me.

Their dark tilium and my pure tilium mixed, and it was like adding vinegar to baking soda. It was explosive! A wave of power shot out from me, and then I felt fire and light streaming from fingers and toes, from my mouth and eyes. The streams of light were a part of me, just another arm or leg.

Then the streams split in half, and then half again. Again and again, they split. Each time, the streams became thinner. Soon, they had split so many times that they'd become thin as spider silk. I could feel every thread, just like they were each a natural part of me.

The threads shot outward from me, racing in every direction. They reached the shell around us, and wherever my threads touched it, the web burned away. In seconds, it looked like Swiss cheese with all the holes burned into it. The burns spread faster and faster, growing. Only a few seconds later, the whole shell exploded into glowing, hot ashes and rained down on us all. The Dark Elves shrieked and fell to the ground, crying out as the falling embers burned them.

"Kill them!" their leader screamed. "Kill the Keepers, now!"

Dark Elves struggled to their feet and staggered toward us. They'd been burned in big splotches over every part of their faces and hands, but they came at us again anyway. It was too bad for them, though, because Jericho and Clara didn't waste any time.

They sprinted toward us even before the ashes finished falling, and they were followed by the dragons and Elves they had come with.

Jericho roared as they sprinted at our attackers. When our cavalry arrived, crashing into the mob of Dark Elves, their leader shot me a last wicked glare like he was wishing I'd just die already, and then leaped through the portal. It closed behind him in a blinding, purple flash.

It didn't take long for Jericho and the others to finish off the Dark Elves who were left behind. A few fought, but most scattered, running in every direction with my rescuers hot on their heels.

Then, I felt like a tub with the stopper pulled out, suddenly empty and my power gone. I crashed to the ground in a heap as I passed out.

***

When I opened my eyes, a dragon in his human form also knelt at my side, watching me. "Welcome back, Keeper," he said. He looked relieved to see me awake.

"Thanks. How long was I out?"

"Maybe ten minutes. We checked you out with my mahier."

I sat up and nodded. A blue dragon, probably. "Thanks." I tried to smile, but it took too much energy, so instead, I looked up into the sky.

The jungle's blackened tree line was like an ugly picture frame for a painting of the most beautiful blue sky I'd ever seen. I wanted to look at that scene forever, but I knew I couldn't. I shook my head to clear it, then looked around. The dragons were piling Dark Elf corpses for the Elves to return to Paraiso for some sort of ceremony. That was their business, though.

Then I noticed Eva, Cairo, Jericho, and Clara huddled together, talking. At least, Jericho was talking, and he was waving his hands around as he let out little puffs of smoke from his nostrils. Just great. I was sure I was about to get chewed out.

I climbed to my feet, and Jericho spotted me. He waved me over, so I braced myself for some yelling and made my feet go in that direction. Instead of flinching, though, I tried to keep my head high.

When I joined the circle, Eva and Cairo smiled. Jericho didn't.

"What in Aprella's name were you thinking, Cole?" More smoke came from his nostrils.

I was almost as afraid of Jericho's legendary temper as I had been of the Dark Elves. I knew it wasn't rational, but Jericho could be really scary when he was mad. "I was thinking that we could learn something about the problem and get one step closer to saving the world. You know, my job."

I saw his fists clench for a second. He said, "Your *job* is to stay alive, both of you, so that you can end the Time of Fear. You aren't the only one who could scout the black spots, but you *are* the only one who isn't expendable."

"Whoa, wait a minute," Eva interrupted. "This was my idea, not Cole's. He came with me because he couldn't stop me, and Cairo came to keep us both safe. Yell at me, not them."

Jericho puffed a smoke ring from his nose, and his eyes flared for a second. "There is plenty of yelling to go around. You were stupid and reckless, Eva, and it almost cost us everything."

He rounded on me again and leaned forward so his face was only a foot from mine. "You want to be a leader? You want to live up to the Keeper of Dragons' role? If you're going to lead us in this war, you need to stop taking stupid risks with your life. A true Keeper needs to make wise decisions. If we can't trust you to be smart with your own life, how is anyone supposed to trust you with theirs? You have to know how to follow before you can lead, boy." He practically spat the last word.

I couldn't meet his gaze anymore. I had to look away. His words stung with the truth.

He stared at me for long seconds before he finally straightened and took a step back. "This isn't over, not for any of you. I can't even deal with whatever you did to take the web shell down. We'll talk about that later. Right now, I can't stand to look at you."

He turned to Cairo and his eyes flared up again. "If you think you can handle doing your job for once, do you think you can get these two back to camp? Try not to let them do anything even stupider on the way home."

With that, he leaped into the air and shifted into his dragon. He was gone in a blink, streaking back to Paraiso. Clara quickly followed him. I was left standing with Cairo and Eva, and they looked as frustrated as I felt.

Eva stepped toward me and raised her hand to put it on my arm, but she must have seen the look on my face because she put her arm down. They stood there, looking at me, at the ground, at each other. It was amazingly awkward for all of us.

Without a word, I jumped up and summoned my dragon, then headed back toward Paraiso The others quickly caught up and flew with me. I didn't say anything, and Eva and Cairo didn't try to make me. They just flew beside me, quietly. I wasn't going very fast, either, since I wasn't looking forward to getting back to camp. They simply just kept pace with me the whole way. I really did appreciate their silent support. I'd have to tell them later, when I felt better.

Along the way, my thoughts were a jumble. Had I really messed up that badly? Considering how close we came to getting captured, we would need to be more careful in the future, but how was I to know the Dark Elves could use the black spots for tilium? Or that they were hunting the Keepers? And I sure couldn't have known about the portal. I'd have to keep that in mind from then on because it meant they could attack us whenever and wherever they wanted.

Or could they only do it when we were in the black spots? Maybe that was the key. We didn't know anything about how it worked or what it was, except that Eldrick caused it by killing off trolls.

But in the end, Jericho's words ran through my mind more than anything else, calling me stupid. The words hurt, but he wasn't wrong. I had led friends far from home and into danger, and we got nothing out of it. All risk, no reward. The more I thought about it, the more I realized the trip really had been stupid, just like Jericho said. He also said a leader couldn't do those things. He was probably right about that, too.

Like a brick hitting me in the head, I realized he was right. I was a terrible leader. I had just figured being the Keeper of Dragons meant that whatever I did, it would come out okay because Fate was on my side. But maybe even Fate couldn't win over bad leadership. And if I couldn't fly over a blackened jungle, how was I supposed to end the war? No, I decided, I was a failure as Keeper of Dragons and a failure as a leader. I'd almost gotten my friends captured or killed, and me along with them.

Ahead, Paraiso came into view. Eva and Cairo both mentioned it telepathically, but I just couldn't bear to reply. I'd let them down so badly, but they wanted to act like everything was okay, like it had just been one bad decision. It wasn't, though. It had been a string of bad decisions, and maybe only Fate kept us alive this long. Luck would run out eventually, though.

Instead of answering them, I banked left to head straight in. I streaked down toward the catwalk outside the room the Elves had given me. Just before landing, I switched into my human, and then I stormed into the room and slammed the door shut behind me. I just couldn't deal with anyone at the moment, and I couldn't bring myself to face any of the people who mattered to me. I threw a lock on the door with my mahier, climbed into bed, and pulled the covers over my face.

In the darkness under the blanket, I finally felt a little better. I lay there for hours, and I could tell when the sun went down because it got even darker under the blanket. Not even Eva tried to visit, which I was thankful for. She knew when to leave me alone.

I didn't know when I fell asleep, but I woke up to a strange sound outside the window. Everything else was silent, and it must have been the middle of the night. As my mind cleared from its sleep fog, I realized the sound was beautiful. If anyone had been with me to hear it, they would probably have said it was *hauntingly* beautiful. To me, it sounded like singing, the prettiest voice I'd ever heard.

I climbed out of bed to look out the window. I had to see what was making such beautiful noise! On the jungle floor was a spot of faint light. It pulsed in time with the singing, getting brighter when the voice rose, fading when it went low and soft. I felt the urge to go meet whoever was down there.

With a flip of my wrist, I made my mahier lock fade away. I didn't bother to fly down, I just "blinked" down the way I'd learned from Gaber when I first got to Paraiso.

When I took a few steps toward the light, it moved away from me. Then it paused. I took another step, and it moved away again. It felt like the singing light wanted me to follow it. Some part of my brain told me I should let someone know where I was going, but it was almost like a trance. I just couldn't bring myself to move away from that beautiful, singing light.

Instead of telling someone, I gave in and followed it. Every step I took, it moved away and then paused. After that, I didn't stop again but sped up. I wanted to catch it. No, I *needed* to catch it.

All thoughts of Paraiso left me, and I began to run.

The Crowns' Accord

Chapter Six

Running through Paraiso, I lost sight of the glow, but I could still hear the singing. Every once in a while, through a row of alley-cropping or between two bigger trees, I'd catch a glimpse of the beautiful glowing thing. It didn't seem to be getting any farther ahead, but I wasn't closing the distance.

I almost ran into an Elf on night watch and shouted an apology over my shoulder as I sprinted onward, leaving him and his surprised expression behind.

Then I bolted down an alleyway between two parallel hedgerows and passed between the two treehouses at the alley's end. I heard the steady, happy murmur of voices talking up above, but I kept running.

Soon, I had settled into a steady pace I could keep up for miles, the same one I used on the obstacle course since no one could sprint forever.

Although it slowed me down, the voice didn't sound like it was getting any farther away. Whatever it was, maybe it had slowed down, too, luring me onward. It had been so beautiful; I simply had to see it again, up close.

I didn't know how long I had been running when I reached Paraiso's edge. The beautiful song ahead of me kept going, so I did as well. I plunged into the jungle, running through its pitch-black undergrowth. I used my mahier senses in a way I never had before—to tell me where the trees were, where I had to jump over a log or duck under a branch. In my head, I was counting my steps with one half of my mind while the other half only thought of the glowing light and its mesmerizing song. I wondered if my heart would feel full if I ever managed to catch it.

Then I heard another voice joining it, a deep sound that seemed to rumble in my chest, and then another voice midway between the deep rumble and the bird-like singing. More voices joined; they blended together and wove a harmony I'd never heard before. It was the most beautiful sound I'd ever heard, or ever would hear again in this lifetime. I forgot all about my steady pace and sprinted forward. I narrowly missed a branch but didn't slow down. I scraped my knee jumping over a log but only put my head down so I could run faster.

The voices grew louder. I was catching up! My beautiful song-light!

Suddenly, I burst through the tree line and found myself in an open field, the stars shining down from above. Here, the moon seemed to bathe everything in a faint glow, like the whole scene had been painted with the most beautiful sparkling paints. Even the rocks had a glowing aura, half mist and half moonlight.

On the far side of that beautiful field, as I became aware of my surroundings again, I saw people. Half a dozen, standing in a semi-circle. One in the middle was motioning me to come toward them. Not only did they each glow softly, but a pillar of cobalt-blue light streaked from each one, shooting into the sky like a spotlight. There were sparkling flecks in that light, like the glitter of a snow globe drifting all through the light and around each person.

I skidded to a halt only a few feet from those strange, glowing people. Somehow, I couldn't sense them with my mahier, like they weren't actually there even though I saw them clearly.

And yet, I knew they weren't there; they were Ancestors. My Ancestors. One was Prince Jago—I had seen him before in a portrait, but the painting didn't do him justice. He was tall and noble, his jaw square and strong, and his eyes glinted with joy as he smiled at me.

When they all stopped singing at once, I felt like something priceless had been ripped out of my heart. I desperately wanted them to sing again but knew they wouldn't because their song had already done its job.

"I don't know how I know it, but you are my Ancestors. And you," I said, looking at Jago, "are my father's brother, who should have been king. But how can you be here?"

The woman next to Jago spoke, and I recognized hers as the first voice I'd heard, the one that had lured me out of Paraiso. My heart leaped with joy at the sound. "We are here to help the Keeper of

Dragons. I think you knew that already, Prince. We have watched you as we sit at Aprella's side. We've seen your struggles, and watched you with pride."

My heart sank. I felt a deep embarrassment, even though I didn't know any of those people. They were spirits, all passed away long before my time, but I desperately wanted their approval. Even so, I had to tell them the truth, though it would be embarrassing and painful, and I worried that they'd turn away from me. But I wouldn't lie.

"We're losing this war. I'm not the leader you need me to be, and I can't drive back the Time of Fear. Eldrick is stronger than me, and the Earth is dying because of it."

Jago said, "You are wrong, Colton. You are the Keeper, and only you can win this war against the evil one. If you fail, the entire Earth will fall. Our strength is in you, though you don't believe it."

The woman next to him added, "If you fail, there will be no hope for dragon kind, for Elves, or for any who follow Truth. You *must* carry on, for yourself and for them."

I felt the weight of their confidence like a ton of gravel poured over me, choking me. I couldn't breathe, I felt trapped. "I can't do it. I told you, I'm not the right one. Why am I the Keeper? Your mistake is going to cost the whole world," I said, my voice cracking.

Jago tilted his head back and laughed into the night, as though what I had said was the funniest thing he'd ever heard. My cheeks flushed with anger, but he held up one hand toward me. "Don't be angry, Prince. If you could know the things I know, you wouldn't feel hopeless. I see strength in you, even if you don't. How else do you think you stole the Farro tilium? How else could you carry the Mere Blade, forged for the Mermaids alone? How did you breathe fire in a day, when other dragons take years? Your questions and mine have the same answer— you were made the Keeper for a reason. Trust in this."

That was a pretty speech, but it didn't convince me. I shook my head without realizing it. In my heart, I knew he was wrong. Making me the Keeper was a mistake, no matter what he said.

As though he could read my thoughts, another man said, "Put your heart at ease. Maybe you haven't been able to stop the growing blackness from arriving, but you have stopped so many things that no one else could have. If you needed a sign, you only have to look at what you've done so far. What you will do in the future is just as grand, so the Fates have spoken. I know you're afraid, but you must fight on. Win or lose, that's all any of us can do, even the Keeper."

I was going to tell him he was wrong again, but then Jago stepped forward. He left the line of my Ancestors, and they watched him with sparkling eyes. I felt like they had hidden smiles behind the glow as they watched him. He stepped up and looked down into my eyes. I could feel his strength radiating.

They should have made him the Keeper.

Jago said, "No, Cole. It wasn't my time, so I must have lacked the strength. I died so the prophecy of the Fates could be fulfilled. So they could find *you*." He reached into the breast pocket of the gorgeous uniform he wore. It was the uniform of Ochana.

When he pulled his hand out, he had something bright shining in it. He turned his hand over and slowly opened his fingers. In his palm was the most beautiful ring I'd ever seen. It was forged in the shape of a dragon, and I thought that if I looked closely enough, I might be able to see every individual scale. I got the impression that it glittered with many colors, even though I could clearly see that it was silver. Two small rubies were set as its eyes, glowing faintly.

Jago said, "This ring is priceless, Nephew. It was forged by the first Dragon Kings and took three generations of dragons to finish. When the time is right, and when your need is most desperate, then you'll see what this ring is for. You alone have the strength and will to use it to summon the ancients to come to your aid."

He held it out, and I let him drop it into my palm. As soon as it touched me, I felt a flood of warmth fill me, and its eyes glowed brightly for a second before slowly fading again.

Without another word, Jago turned around and walked back to the line. They all stood looking at me, smiling as they slowly faded away. When they were gone, the pillars of light were gone, too, and the field didn't glow anymore. It was just an ordinary, star-lit clearing in the jungle at night, and I was alone.

I dropped the ring into my shirt pocket. Then I heard a rustling sound behind me. An enemy must've followed the lights! I spun around and crouched as I drew the Mere Blade, a snarl on my face, ready to fight whatever Dark Elves or Carnites had found me.

Instead of an enemy, though, I saw Eva stepping out from the bushes, her eyes as wide as saucers.

Chapter Seven

I think my eyes went as wide as Eva's when I spotted her hiding in the bushes. "What are you doing there? And— "

"—and how long have I been here?" she asked, finishing my sentence for me. "When I saw you running through Paraiso, I decided to follow you. Just to make sure you were okay."

"How much did you see?"

She looked down at the ground as she bit her lower lip, avoiding my eyes suddenly. Her silence spoke volumes.

I said, "Okay. You saw everything, then. Are you going to tell anyone?" I wasn't sure why I didn't want her to say anything, but I had the urge to tell her to keep it to herself.

"You mean, am I going to tell Jericho that his best friend and the Ancestors had a concert in the jungle and gave you door prizes? No, I don't think so. For some reason, it feels like it should be private."

I nodded. I felt sort of the same way about it, actually. "I don't know why I followed the singing, but it was almost like it put me in a trance and I had to follow. I was as surprised as anyone to find myself talking to ghosts. How do you think they were able to give me something? You know, something physical?"

"I don't know. Jericho might know if you told him. The glow-peeps were right about you, you know. You're a lot stronger than you think you are. I've always seen it in you, even if you didn't."

It was my turn to look away. "The last thing I want is more people telling me how great I am. I'm here and fighting, but let's just leave it at that."

She was quiet for a minute and stared at me, looking me in the eyes like she was thinking about challenging me again. Instead, she said, "Can I see the ring? I didn't get a good look at it, before."

I hesitated. I wasn't sure why. Or maybe I just didn't want to find a ring in my pocket, proving the whole thing had been real. At last, though, I handed it to her.

"Thanks," she said as she examined the ring in the moonlight. "You see how it sort of shimmers? It's like it's glowing, like the moonlight makes it stronger. Or maybe we can only see its power in the moonlight."

"How do you know? Maybe it glows in the daytime, too."

She shrugged. "Maybe. Either way, I think you should wear it. Whatever this thing is, it has to be special for your Ancestors to come and give it to you personally, and if you're wearing it, you can't lose it. You need to take good care of this, Cole. I have a feeling it's going to be important."

I took the ring back from her and held it in my palm. As I moved it around, examining it, I again saw the echo of different colors in it, and no matter how I turned it, I felt like its two little ruby eyes followed me. I was trying to build up the courage to put it on because she was right—it would be safer if I wore it. I couldn't lose it if it were on me.

At last, I took a deep breath and slid the ring on my right ring finger. It felt warm and comforting for a moment, but then there was a flash of light that dazzled me, and the ring disappeared. I gasped and looked closely at my fingers. That's when I saw that it hadn't disappeared. Not quite. I could see a shape on my finger, under the skin, that looked kind of like the dragon from the ring.

She gasped. "It's like it merged with you. It's a part of you now."

"I hope that's a good thing," I said. It still felt warm, even under my skin. Whatever fears I had about the ring faded away.

She stepped up beside me and slid her arm around mine, joined at our elbows. She looked up at me and smiled. "Let's get back to bed. Maybe we can catch a couple hours of sleep before Jericho starts in on us again bright and early."

I was suddenly exhausted, and sleep sounded like a great idea. "Okay. I don't know about you, but I'm wiped out."

We walked back to Paraiso arm in arm, neither one saying anything, just being there together. It was enough for the moment since neither of us knew if we'd get to do that again in this lifetime. I was glad to have a good friend like her, for however long I kept us alive.

***

"And... Stop," Jericho called out.

Dripping sweat, I climbed to my feet from the side-straddle-hops we had been doing for the last few minutes. It was just the latest torture he inflicted on us. The other trainees and I waited for the next command. While we waited, we rolled our shoulders or stretched our necks.

Suddenly, Jericho was right in front of me. I jumped a little, startled. He shouted right in my face, "Did I tell you to move around? No. I said stop. That means you get in the position of attention. Now drop and give me fifty push-ups."

I glanced at Eva and the others, who definitely weren't at the "position of attention" either.

Eva shrugged and looked confused.

Jericho, still inches from my face, shouted, "Did I tell you to eyeball them? Is that part of the position of attention? No. That's ten more push-ups. Get on your face! Do it now!"

That was totally unfair. The others were still moving around, not at the "POA," but they weren't getting extra pushups. Come to think of it, all the training that morning had been me getting the short end of the stick from Jericho's unwelcome attentions. I dropped down and started pumping out push-ups. When I got to sixty, I climbed to my feet. After that, though, I made sure to stand at attention. I was the only one doing it, but so what.

Jericho marched back and forth in front of our lineup, his hands behind his back, and glared at us one at a time. I thought we'd get in more trouble, but he didn't say anything about how some of the others were slouching. My irritation started turning into something a bit stronger.

He shouted to us, "Partner up for sit-ups. You'll do it until you knock out eighty of them, then switch. *Prince Colton*, since you feel like eyeballing me, you'll do one-hundred sit-ups. Ready, begin."

The others dropped to the ground, but I didn't move. Forget this guy. I'd had more than enough. Why was he picking on me? I glared at him, trying not to say what I really wanted to say. It wouldn't have been polite, that was for sure.

Of course, in a flash, Jericho was right in front of me again, yelling in my face, his eyes glowing red, but he was so mad that he wasn't making sense. His words came out all jumbled. Whatever side of the bed he woke up on that morning, he didn't have to take it out on me. As he shouted, an image went through my mind of a chicken with red eyes, head bobbing as it clucked angrily.

The image made me laugh, and Jericho's expression at that made me laugh even harder. The jerk was a chicken, clucking at the dog like it was in charge! I couldn't help it. I tried to stop laughing but I couldn't.

Jericho froze mid-shout. He stepped up to me, so close that his face was only a breath from mine.

I tried not to laugh again, but a burst of air came out from between my tightly pressed lips, and his nose-smoke blew away. "Lose your bearing, *Prince*?

Are you just stupid, or don't you care if everyone around you is stronger and faster than you are? Maybe you don't care how many people have to die saving you because you're too precious to do a sit-up. I'm sure they won't mind carrying your load, too. Need a rest-break, do we?"

I knew he was just trying to make me mad, but it worked. I clenched my fists and almost took a swing at him, but stopped myself at the last moment. He looked like he was expecting me to.

His lip curled. "You feel like taking a swing at your commanding officer, do you? But you expect these people to follow you someday? Fine, I'll give you the chance to take your best shot. Go ahead—swing at me."

I didn't move. Was he serious? I couldn't tell for sure. I really wanted to take him up on that, though.

He turned to the others, who were on the ground doing sit-ups or just sitting there staring at Jericho and me, and he said, "On your feet, trainees. Pair off for quarterstaff training."

He turned back to me and leaned in so that his mouth was inches from my ear. "If you think you're ready to take a swing at me, do it out there. Let's see what you really got, *kid*."

I thought if I stepped into the square with him, one of us would get hurt. I truly wanted to beat the smug look off his face with a big stick. I didn't know why he was picking on me, and I didn't care. But I knew better than to take him up on his offer. "No. Go fight yourself, Jericho." I put the emphasis on the last word like it was an insult.

He froze, eyes locked with mine. I think he was stunned silent for once. Good. I was tired of the sound of his stupid voice.

I said, "I'm done getting your special treatment. Get out of my face, or I'm going to do something only one of us is going to feel bad about later."

He took a step back, mouth gaping open. After a second, his mouth snapped shut with a click. He said, "This training is going to save your life, Cole. Now get over there and—"

"No," I shouted, loud enough for everyone else to hear. "What's the point of all this training? I won't win anyway."

"You're the Keeper of Dragons. Of course, you'll win. I expect your best efforts—"

"Everyone expects things from me. You just don't get it!"

I felt my eyes burning and my throat got tight. I said, "I'm going to let everyone down. And the cherry on top is, I get to have you bully me in front of everyone. Maybe you just like tearing down what you'll never be, though. A *prince*." I glared at him, practically daring him to say something.

I felt a hand on my shoulder. It was Eva. Very quietly, she said, "The Ancestors. Tell him, Cole, and—"

Jericho interrupted and hissed at her, "What about the Ancestors? Speak more sense than this half-wit."

I couldn't take it anymore. I just kept getting angrier, and none of it was fair. What did they want from me? Save the world. Yeah, right. I was just eighteen, a baby in dragon years. Snapping, I knocked Eva's hand off my shoulder and spun to yell at her, too. But when I saw the hurt, scared look on her face, that was the last straw. She was disappointed in me, too.

I had to get out of there. I turned on my heels and ran. I poured all my anger into running, and it felt good. I kept running, faster and faster, and my rage kept growing. How dare they! I wanted to break things, destroy things, smash Jericho's smug face into the ground.

Behind me, Eva and Jericho both yelled for me to stop, and with my mahier senses, I felt them chasing me, but I also felt their concern and worry wash over me.

Suddenly, I didn't feel angry anymore. It drained away, and all I felt was embarrassed. I had thrown a tantrum, but they still came after me and worried. I couldn't face them, so I ran harder.

I dodged through bushes and over logs, jumped across a creek without slowing down, and soon found myself deep in the jungle. My senses told me they were getting farther behind, and when they came to the creek, they slowed down just enough for me to get a really good lead on them.

In a couple more seconds, they were too far away for me to sense them anymore. Still I kept running. It felt good. Everything I was angry or scared of came pouring out, fueling my legs to go faster and faster, ignoring the burn. I started to feel better than I had in a long time, actually. I came to a decision then, and it was like a huge weight lifting off my shoulders.

I must have run at least a couple more miles like that at a dead sprint, my mahier fueling my muscles, when I came to the gray edge of blackness deep in the jungle. The gray outside edge was closer to Paraiso than it had been the last time I saw it. Jericho didn't want me anywhere near the Congo's black areas, but I smirked and decided that was all the more reason to keep going. Yeah! I'd go in and find a way to fix the jam we were all in, whether he wanted me to or not.

In a moment, I'd passed through the gray and was into the black. I stopped running and looked around. All that blackness made me feel sad. The Congo had been so beautiful and green, not long ago. Before it got painted black.

My senses told me the entire region had no tilium in it. I didn't feel even a trace of mahier, either. Surely, if any animals and insects were still in there, I'd have felt something, even just a twinkle?

But I felt nothing. Out of curiosity, I tried to draw in mereum, the power of the mermaids. The Queen had told me that even air had mereum in it, riding in the humidity. Anything with a trace of water had mereum, even people and animals.

I still sensed nothing! I had no idea how that could be. There was water in the dirt and the air. There had to even be some moisture in the blackened trees, or they'd just be a pile of dust, I thought. But no mahier, no tilium, no mereum.

An idea hit me. It probably wouldn't work, but it was worth a try. Nothing else had worked, so why not? I reached my hand out over a blackened bush, standing about knee high. My mahier and tilium charges were still full, and I was close enough to the green to draw mereum from there. I focused on long, slow, and even breaths, and felt my heartbeat settle down from the long run. I started to pull in mereum. Suddenly, I got a buzzing feeling in my head—not painful, but not comfortable. Once before, I had mixed my mahier and the tilium I took from the Farro. It had purified their dark tilium into something new—my own pure tilium.

My idea was something I had never tried before. I didn't know what would happen if I pulled my mereum into that pure tilium. I was the only dragon who could use mereum who wasn't a mermaid. I couldn't use it well, but I could gather it in with my other powers, at least.

I felt the three powers swishing around inside me, and I stretched my hand out over the blackened little shrub and closed my eyes. With my mahier senses, I could still see the bush in my mind's eye, a gray outline against a field of white. In the healthy jungles, all I would have seen was green. I thought the white might mean that the land wasn't poisoned by adding something new, but instead, it may have just been stripped of every kind of energy.

Slowly, I reached out with my mahier, the power of dragons, the power of Truth. Then, I reached out with my purified tilium, the power of life and nature. Nothing happened, and the little bush stayed black.

It was time to try my idea. I thought about my mereum flowing out of me, through my hand, and into the plant. Mereum was the power of water, the irresistible force that could even carve away rock over time.

I felt it mix with mahier and tilium, and as soon as they touched, the mereum was absorbed into my tilium like water into a sponge. Water and life were so closely related, I didn't know if I was even surprised at the reaction.

Then, my mahier begin to wind its way through the new energy, whatever mereum and tilium became together. Tendrils of mahier spread through the bush, like fiberglass holding two sheets together and making both stronger. Then the new energy mix flowed around the bush. It settled over every leaf, and I could feel it going down into the roots, and then into the dirt and roots under it. I kept the energy flowing, but I opened my eyes to look.

My eyes went wide with surprise—the bush was green again! I didn't need my dragon senses to see that the leaves had turned green, then the stems turned from black to properly brown from the top to the bottom, and when it touched the soil, black and gray vanished. All that was left behind was rich, brown, healthy soil. Even the fallen leaves and other debris that covered the dirt weren't blackened anymore. They went from black to brown, like dead leaves should be, but then they turned green again! My jaw dropped as I felt dead bugs and earthworms twitch and come to life.

I wished Eva were there. It was incredible, stunning, and totally cool. *I could restore balance to the Earth!*

Chapter Eight

I stood looking at the little bit of green, the tiny island of life that I'd restored. My heart pounded in my ears from the excitement of realizing the world wasn't doomed. Somehow, I'd gathered all three kinds of power. Maybe the energy harmonized and made the whole thing stronger, different—like a fourth power no one had ever seen before.

And it could save a dying world!

I heard people rustling behind me, but in that almost lifeless place, I could sense their energy clearly. It was Jericho, with Eva and Cairo. I didn't turn around, too thrilled at the little patch of life to care about getting chewed out.

Footsteps, and then Jericho shouted at me with iron in his voice, "What are you thinking, Cole? Do you have any idea how worried we were or the danger you put yourself in? You put all of us in danger, too. We had to chase you through the blackness. Reckless! Do you have any idea what happens if they kill you?"

I turned to face them, but I just couldn't wipe the grin off my face. I think it surprised them all because they looked stunned. Eva's face went from just mad to both mad and smirking.

"What are you smiling at, fool?" Jericho shouted at me, his eyes glowing red and smoke puffing from his nose. "Don't you get—"

Still grinning, I cut him off. "Look," I said, and stepped aside to show the green life I'd brought back. "See what I did?"

His eyes went wide as he realized what he was looking at. Stunned, he looked up into my eyes. "You did that?"

Cairo's mouth was open, both eyebrows raised high on his forehead, and Eva stepped around us to get a look at the green island in the ocean of black all around it.

"Yes," I replied, and grinned even wider. "It's not too late for the world. I figured out how to save it. I had to use all the magic I could—dragon, Elven, Mermaid. I don't know why, but it worked."

"By Aprella's eyes, this is a miracle," Jericho said, and his nose stopped puffing smoke. "You can heal the plants? How did you know what to do?"

"It just came to me. I poured all my energy into it and willed the plant to heal. And even the dirt went back to a normal, healthy brown."

Jericho shoved his fist into the air for a second, like he'd just scored a touchdown. "Yes! I can't believe it, Cole. You figured it out! The Keeper of Dragons will save the world, just like the prophecy says." Then he fist-pumped the air again.

He clapped me on the shoulder, and Cairo shook my hand, both grinning like fools just like me, but Eva said, "That's great." I could tell from her tone that there was a "but" coming along with it.

Sure enough, she continued, "But there's a huge difference between sprucing up this little plant and healing the Earth."

The three of us went silent and turned to stare at her like she was a Martian, or like she'd grown another head.

She shook her head at us. "Look at me like that if you want, but Cole is just one dragon. Maybe he can keep Paraiso green, but the blackness is *spreading*, and faster than he can heal it. So, it's just not going to be enough, is it?"

She froze, waiting for him to reply, and I think she was desperate to hear she was wrong. The problem was, she wasn't. How long had it taken me to heal one plant? The black had to have covered more area on Earth than I healed, just in the time it took me to do it.

At last, Jericho shook his head just a little bit and looked down at the little plant. It was already less green than it had been when I healed it. It would be dead again soon. He finally said, "Come on. We need to get back to Paraiso and share the news. Maybe Gaber or the fairy queen will have ideas on what to do once they learn about this. There's got to be a way we can take advantage of this discovery, even if we don't know it yet."

We walked side by side through the black, dead Congo, talking mostly about happier days ahead once we figured out how to cure the world. It was a nice thought, at least.

***

As we were walking back, Eva and I found ourselves side by side at one point. She looked so sad. I walked next to her, to be there for her if she wanted to talk, trying to simply give her silent support.

After an awkward minute, she said, "You know I'm sorry, right? Everyone was so happy, maybe I should have just waited to say anything. I feel bad."

That was my friend Eva. She was as strong as anyone I ever knew, and it always surprised me to hear her doubts when she was usually so fearless. "Hey, don't apologize. Nothing you said could take away how awesome it felt to bring that plant back. So it won't heal the whole planet. It's a start, right? We know more now than we did before. Someone will have an idea how we can use it, so cheer up," I teased her, smiling so she knew I wasn't upset. "For the first time, I really feel like maybe things are looking up, like Fate didn't make some horrible mistake picking us."

She didn't say anything. She just slid her arm around my waist as we walked, and I thought she looked a bit happier. More relaxed.

It wouldn't last.

To my right, there were sudden noises in the black jungle, like trees falling. I stepped away from Eva, putting myself between her and the sounds just by reflex. I reached out with my senses, then felt something out there. I focused hard on it, but I couldn't get a solid impression. It was like catching glimpses of a light through trees, never there long enough to see what it was. "I can't feel it," I said, looking at Jericho. "Something is out there, but I can't get a grip on it."

He nodded, staring out into the jungle. He was concentrating, too, but the noise was getting closer. When he drew his sword, so did the rest of us. "Be ready, and if that's not just a herd of duikers, run."

I got ready to run. That seemed likely, since the deer-like duikers didn't travel in herds and, being dog-sized, wouldn't knock over even blackened trees. "Eva, I'll follow you if we have to run for our lives."

Interestingly, we all moved into pairs without anyone telling us to. Jericho and I stood back to back, while Eva and Cairo did the same. We had barely gotten into position when whatever was crashing through the jungle reached the edge of the little clearing we stood in. They didn't even slow down—at least half a dozen Carnites burst from the tree line.

I didn't have time to think about it because the Carnites reached us in only a few of their giant steps. In the daytime, here in the open, the things looked just as terrifying as they did at night, but none of these had their usual tree-trunk clubs. Instead, four had what looked like nets, while two had long, thin trees stripped of any branches which they held out with the tips toward us like spears. They broke off into two equal groups, forcing each of us to face a Carnite with a net, and each pair had a spear guy. The way they surrounded us made it impossible to run. Usually, Carnites just charged right at anything that moves, but not these.

My Carnite threw his net at me, but I knocked it aside with my mahier shield. Then one with a spear stabbed at me. The blunt tip hit me in the shoulder and sent me spinning to the ground. It felt like a massive hammer blow. I couldn't believe how strong one Carnite was.

The net came again, spreading out as it flew toward me, and I frantically rolled aside. That left me and Jericho both fighting alone.

As I scrambled to my feet, Jericho was spinning out of the way of another net, and we made eye contact for a split second. I glanced at Eva and Cairo; they had also been split up. This wasn't going well. At this rate, they'd kill us all.

Eva faced another Carnite, ready to knock aside its net, but she didn't see the one behind her. I sprinted toward her and, holding my mahier shield out in front of me, leaped through the air. I knocked the big net away enough that it missed her, and when I hit the ground, I tucked my chin and rolled into a somersault, then came up on my feet again.

"I can't hold them off!" Eva cried.

No kidding. It was pretty clear we were done for. I just couldn't get close enough with my sword to get at them, not with the spear-wielding Carnites keeping us away from the ones with the nets.

Then Jericho's clear warrior voice rose over the noise of battle. "To the north. Run! I'll make an opening."

I dodged another net, leaping aside and landing on my shoulder with a thud. It hurt, but I got to my feet without missing a beat. "What about you?" I couldn't leave him there, and I didn't want him to do something stupid. Of course, staying there to get killed or caught sounded pretty stupid, too.

He shouted, "By Aprella, do as I say, kid. Follow me!"

I turned and headed north, sprinting. It wasn't time to argue about being called a kid. Cairo ran next to me, and Eva was just behind him.

Jericho was five steps ahead of all of us. As we headed north, only two net throwers attacked us, the other two being somewhere between us and freedom, but both spear Carnites were to either side. One thrust its tree at me, but I ducked and the spear passed inches over my head.

Just before Jericho reached the two surprised-looking Carnites ahead of us, he leaped into the air and summoned his dragon faster than I had ever seen anyone do before. With his wings spread out, he crashed into the giant Carnites, and all three went down to the ground in a tangle of arms, legs, and wings.

The rest of us leaped over the twisting pile and then reached the tree line. We ran into the jungle. We were clear! "Keep running!" I shouted.

I didn't look to see if they were following me, but I could hear footsteps behind me and was glad they listened. As I ran, I began frantically thinking about how best to gather up a rescue party. I had to find Gaber first, and then we could—

I saw a shadow to my left and felt the air move, but I didn't have time to realize what was happening before a Carnite, still chasing us, backhanded me like he was swinging at a golf ball. I flew through the air until I hit a tree and bounced off, only to land on the ground on my back. I went into panic mode, not thinking at all, just rolled over and used my hands to push up enough to get my feet under me. Then I was off and running.

A second later, I risked glancing around me but I didn't see Eva or Cairo. I was alone, and we had been scattered in the jungle, being chased by Carnites. It didn't look good. I had to find them.

"Eva!" I shouted as loudly as I could while sprinting through a dense, dark jungle. There was no reply, but right away, the crashing sounds of two Carnites changed directions and then grew louder. Argh! I'd drawn their attention, but maybe it would give the others a better chance at getting away.

The Carnites were getting closer, even though I was siphoning my mahier into running. No human could have kept up, I think, but Carnites were big and fast. A net flew at me from my right, and I knocked it aside with my shield, but sprinting as I was, the movement knocked me off balance. I tripped and the ground rushed up at me. I landed hard, but I was already scrambling to my feet by the time I slid to a stop.

I never got the chance to take off running again. Another net came at me from the other side, and there was nothing I could do to avoid it. It hit me dead-center and knocked me to the ground. I struggled, but yet another net landed on me and I got completely entangled.

I only hoped Eva had escaped.

Chapter Nine

I struggled to find the nets' edges to escape, but before I could, one of the giant Carnites sprinted right at me. I thought it was going to trample me. I curled into a ball and covered my head with my arms. It didn't stomp on me, though. Instead, at the last minute, it bent down and swooped up the net in one hand, bringing me up with it like potatoes in a weave sack. It held me up in the air and brought the bag close to its face. I wanted to jam the Mere Blade into its stupid, ugly eyes, but the net had me pinned so I couldn't get the sword free.

The hideous thing had two long, sharp tusks jutting up from its mouth, which was as wide as its pig-like face, but its skin was sickly pale like moonlight and looked kind of like cottage cheese with the way it puckered and bunched up into rolls and pits. I could see little open sores all over its body, and it smelled bad enough to knock over a horse.

As it looked at me with its beady little eyes, its nostrils—just two holes in its face, really, since it didn't have a nose to speak of—flared open, and it hit me with a gust of breath as it snorted. The hot, foul breath smelled like rotting meat in a sauna, and I had to fight not to retch. It opened its mouth and lowered me, net and all, snapping its teeth at me.

That's when I panicked. Even more than I had before. All I could think of was getting away as I struggled inside the net, desperate, but the ropes were too thick and tight. It was going to swallow me, net and all.

I shrieked, screaming at the top of my lungs.

The Carnite pulled the bag away from its face and made a disgusting, wet-sounding grunting noise over and over, and I realized it was laughing at me. I stared at the monster, wishing I could somehow get to it with my sword.

The other Carnite walked up to it, and the two beasts sniffled and snorted at each other. They sounded angry, at least to me. I didn't know if

Carnites were ever anything but angry. After a moment, though, they both turned west. The one holding me tied the sack to its belt, really just a few ropes woven together and tied at the waist. Every time it took one of its long steps, I was bashed around, bouncing off its thigh. I grabbed onto the net and held on for dear life, even though there was no way I would fall with it tied to the belt.

Where were these brutal Carnites taking me? From what I heard, Carnites weren't good for anything but fighting and breaking things. To them, every problem was a nail, and they were the hammer. Using nets, leaving people alive, even working in a team the way they had was all just so weird. The only explanation was that somebody was controlling them, and it wouldn't take three guesses to figure out who was doing it.

The trees went by as the monsters calmly walked away, tearing me from my life with the Elves and dragons. Who knew how my friends would do without me, without the Keeper of Dragons? I felt certain that King Eldrick would win, and the Earth would be lost. All the Elves and dragons, Trolls and

Fairies—everyone who believed in Truth—all would soon be dead or slaves.

My eyes watered up and overflowed, and I quietly cried for the first time in I didn't know how long.

The giant Carnite had taken half a dozen pounding, bone-jarring steps when I heard a high-pitched scream. Then the monster began to fall, toppling like a tree, and the ground rushed up at me. I barely had time to throw up a mereum cushion to soften my landing, but it still knocked the wind out of me.

As I lay bound inside the net, trying to get my breath back, I heard the other Carnite fighting someone. It only lasted a few seconds before that monster roared in anger, then that scary noise got cut short mid-scream. My first thought was that the other Carnites had started a fight with my two, trying to get more spoils to take back to Eldrick, but then a familiar face came into view above me, peering down at me.

"You okay?" Eva asked. "I don't see any blood on you. We need to go save the others. Can you get out of that net?"

I shook my head, feeling light-headed from not being able to breathe. I was just able to sip the air a bit, but at least it was coming back to me. She took out her dagger and furiously worked to cut through the thick ropes of my net. It didn't take long to cut enough to let me wiggle my way out.

Thankfully, my breath was coming back, too. It wasn't the first time I'd had the wind knocked out of me, and I hated it every time. It hurt and it was a little scary. "Thanks for coming to my rescue," I said, looking at the two dead Carnites. At least she'd finished them off quickly. They might have been monsters, but I didn't like to see even them suffering

Eva grinned. "I guess that makes you the damsel in distress, huh? Cairo and Jericho both got captured, and their Carnites headed off that way," she said as she pointed west. "I don't know why the monsters split up, but I think they just didn't want to share the credit for capturing us."

I stretched my arms and rolled my shoulders a couple times to make sure I wasn't hurt worse than I'd thought. Then, Eva and I ran the way she'd pointed. She set a fast pace, but not sprinting. It was a speed we could keep up for a few miles and still fight. Maybe fifteen minutes later, I caught sight of the black trees up ahead swaying, like in that old movie about cloned dinosaurs getting loose and running around on a jungle island.

"There they are," I said, panting.

She nodded, then put her head down and ran faster, pulling ahead. I sped up, too, and drew the Mere Blade as we approached. Neither of us said a word before we jumped into the fight, and we dropped two Carnites before they even knew what hit them. The other two backed off, probably just surprised, but that was a mistake because the two we had taken out first were carrying Jericho and Cairo. We cut them out of their net in seconds, and then the two Carnites faced four of us. They turned and ran.

Eva started to run after them, but Jericho shouted, "Leave them."

Frustrated, she stomped back to us shouting, "Rats! Do you realize this is, like, the third time someone tried to catch us? Why aren't they trying to kill us? I wanted to question those two."

Jericho didn't flinch or step back from Eva raging in his face. Calmly, he said, "Do you speak Carnite?"

She paused, and I watched her closely. I wasn't sure if I should be amused or concerned about what she'd do. But instead of shouting again, she looked away and shook her head.

I asked, "Do they even talk?"

Jericho smiled at me but didn't take his eyes off of Eva. "Yes, a little bit. You heard one talk a long time ago, the first time you met one. But even if any of us knew their language, I don't think they'd trust us with any useful information. Eldrick's forces seem like they're trying to kidnap dragons. Not just us, but every dragon they find."

My eyes went wide in surprise. "What? Why would they do that?" My mind raced, but I didn't come up with anything that made sense. I also didn't know why he'd kept that news to himself.

Eva clenched her jaw and, between her gritted teeth, she asked, "What purpose does that serve? It's the Keepers they need to stop if they want to win, and Eldrick already started the dying Earth by killing Trolls. I doubt dragons dying would do that, or you'd know it."

"Well, that is indeed a question, isn't it? But I may have an idea. I need you kids to go—"

Eva cut him off. "What idea? You can't say that and then just send us back to camp without telling us what's going on. And we aren't kids anymore."

Jericho paused like he was thinking about it, but then he gave her a faint shake of his head. "No, not until I know for sure. And I know you aren't truly kids anymore. Children don't defeat Carnites. But you can't help me with this one. I need to go look into some things, then I'll tell you."

He turned to Cairo and said, "Get the Keepers back to Paraiso safely. Don't let them wander anywhere else alone, got it?"

Cairo gave him the dragons' salute, but Jericho was already mid-shift into his dragon form, rising into the air, and he left us behind. I couldn't help but smile a little bit when he left, too.

"All right, let's get back to camp," Cairo said. "We have to warn everyone about the Carnites, and my telepathy hasn't been working well in all this black stuff."

We walked in silence toward the Elves' home. Eva was angry still at being called a child, but I was too busy thinking to deal with that, and she wasn't the only one with hurt feelings. Plus, Cairo had been right about the mind-talk not working well out there. I tried sending my thoughts to Eva, but if she heard me, she didn't respond.

The Crowns' Accord

Chapter Ten

Jericho was gone, which made me happy, even a little giddy. Good riddance. In my head, I knew how important he was and how much he did for Ochana, but I didn't always *like* him. Lately, he'd made it pretty hard to remember he was on my side. It sure didn't feel like he was.

The black jungle was giving into gray, which boosted my mood a bit more, too. "So, what do you think that was all about?" I asked as we made our way between some ashy-looking trees.

Eva grunted, climbing over a log in our way. "Good question. I hope he's okay. I don't know, though."

I didn't care if he was okay or not. That wasn't really true, I did want him to be okay. But I was still mad at him. Maybe if he just got some scrapes and a bruised ego...

Cairo said, "I don't know, but if he can get Eldrick to quit trying to capture you two, I'll be thrilled. I don't like not knowing what's going on. At least if they attacked us, I could understand that. Killing each other, I get. Kidnapping? It's just weird. Carnites don't take prisoners."

"They do now," Eva replied. "While he's gone, we should try to figure out the source of whatever spell is killing everything. Maybe we could deal with that, one problem at a time."

I snorted. "Jericho is the problem. He treats us like kids, then leaves us alone in the jungle while he runs off chasing his tail. Are we kids, or aren't we? Make up your mind, Mr. High-and-Mighty. How are we supposed to fix anything if he doesn't tell us what's going on?"

"Oh, behave," Cairo said. His voice sounded like eyes rolling. "Jericho puts Ochana before everything else, including himself, and it's not right for you to forget that. He's gruff and mean, but he has a lot of weight on his shoulders. I know he's hard to deal with, though." His voice pitched higher a bit at the end.

"Yeah, I guess. But he doesn't have to treat everyone like that." I kicked a little rock, and it went flying into the gray, dark underbrush.

Eva said, "No, he doesn't have to, but we have bigger things to worry about. Like where the magic is coming from. Any idea where to look?"

My ears perked up. Adventure sounded better than sitting around waiting for Jericho! "No, not really."

Cairo said, "The Earth started getting black spots when Eldrick killed the Trolls, so maybe King Evander knows where to start looking."

I clenched my jaw and took a deep breath to squash my frustration. "The Troll King isn't here, plus I don't think he'll talk to us. Dragons let his Troll-kin get captured, then let them get killed."

"Evander isn't the only Troll left. I bet we can find others in Paraiso. They can't *all* blame us for Eldrick's actions, so maybe we can get one of them to talk to us."

As soon as we got back, we started looking for Trolls. The first man I spoke to didn't even reply, he just kept walking like I was invisible. Eva tried with the next one we saw, but that troll said she didn't know anything. She also kept looking around, like she was afraid to be seen with us.

After she had walked off, I said, "Let's go by the lake. Trolls liked to hang out on the shore sometimes, away from the training grounds."

We pushed our way through the underbrush to the water, then worked our way around the shoreline. Eva was the first to spot another troll, a woman sitting on a rock near the water with her knees tucked up to her chin and her arms wrapped around her legs.

Eva walked up, smiling. "Hi, how's the water?"

The Troll didn't smile back. "You know we don't swim in it. That's Elf Ancestor water."

I stepped up beside Eva and waved. "Of course. Eva's not good at breaking the ice, so I'm sorry about that. It's just a figure of speech anyway."

She nodded, then looked back out over the water and said, "No offense taken, dragons."

When she didn't say anything else, I blurted, "Why won't you Trolls talk to us?"

Cairo shot me a glare, but the Troll looked sideways at me. "You know why. Just because we know you didn't hold the knife yourselves doesn't mean things are okay between our people. The Trolls are hurt, scared, and angry. Maybe you know how that feels?"

Actually, I did know how that felt. The memory of meeting my parents, Rylan and Sila, came to mind. I hadn't been very easy on them at first, for the very same reason. "I can understand that. But you're talking to us, at least. Thanks for that. You know, I was wondering—"

Eva elbowed me in the ribs. "We."

"*We* were wondering... Do you have any idea what kind of spell is making the jungle turn black? I know how Eldrick started it, but do you know why it worked or why it kept going after the rest of the Trolls were rescued?"

She stared over the cerulean water, utterly still. In the water, the reflection of her and her rock under that sky was like a mirror image. It was beautiful. "I never thought about it. I figured if anyone knew why, they'd say so. Haven't you been out there to look?"

Cairo said, "Yes, we have. It just didn't work. Since you're a Troll and it started with the Trolls, do you have any ideas?"

She took a deep breath, then stretched out her legs before hopping off her rocky perch. "I guess we should start by going out there. Maybe if I look at it, since I'm a Troll, I might see something you missed, or feel something different."

I nodded. That was a good idea. Even if it didn't work, it was still better than sitting around waiting for Jericho to get back to bellowing orders at us. And it was time we could spend trying to mend things between dragons and Trolls.

She led us all away from the lake, but not the direction I'd expected.

I said, "The black jungle is that way."

"Actually, it's all around us. There's a patch over here that's closest."

"Cool," I said, and we followed her. A couple minutes later, I saw the blackness ahead. It looked thick, like oil covering everything instead of just color fading out like in the other places. "I didn't know this was here."

The troll shook her head. "It wasn't here until this morning sometime. It just popped up. I've stayed away from it since then." She walked to the edge of the black, then stopped and closed her eyes. After a moment, she said, "I don't sense anything in there."

"Same for us," I said. "Inside the black, it's not just like something is missing. It's more like the nothing is its own thing."

She nodded and snapped her fingers. "Yes! But it can't really be empty. Maybe if I step into it and then try to sense it."

I held out my arm to the black, inviting her to try. What could it hurt?

She took a couple steps beyond the edge until she stood entirely within the blackness. She bent down and closed her eyes, then reached her fingertips down to touch the black, leafy jungle floor. "I'm not sure, but I—"

She shrieked and fell to the ground, then kept screaming. Her eyes rolled up in her head, and she started to convulse. Her whole body shook.

Just as my shock wore off, I took a step toward her, but she shrieked again and her whole body went rigid. Her back arched so badly that she only touched the ground at her heels and the back of her head. That scream sounded like my worst nightmares.

Before I even thought about the risk, I wrapped one arm around her and lifted her off the ground, and ran back to the green. She shrieked the whole time. Cairo grabbed her feet and we carried her out of the dead spot.

We set her down on the green jungle floor just as Elves arrived. They must have heard the screaming. How could they miss it, though, when she was still shrieking?

The Elves coming through the jungle took one look at what was happening and their leader pointed a spear at us. "King Gaber's hat! What have you dragons done?" His pupils were wide open, taking in every bit of jungle light, and his lip curled back to bare his teeth at us.

"Nothing! She went into the dark spot, and when she touched the ground, she collapsed. Help her!" I didn't care about being blamed. The Troll needed help.

Four more Elves poured around the first, two shoving Cairo and me aside while the other two grabbed the Troll. Her body was flopping like a fish out of water when they got her arms around their shoulders and rushed back toward Paraiso, dragging her between them.

As the leader turned away, I asked, "Will she be okay? I only—"

"Silence! I don't care what you were *only* doing. Gaber was a fool to trust you."

I stepped forward, ignoring his spear tip, determined to follow the others. "Forget about that. Will she be okay?"

The Elf blocked my way with his spear. "Stay away from her, *dragon*. We'll take your latest victim to the medical ward. Get back to your quarters and stay there! If you try to leave, Keepers or not, I'll have you in chains. Gaber isn't here to save you." His face was a mask of snarling anger, and I could only nod once, shocked. He spun on his heels and stormed after his companions.

What else was there to do? I looked at Eva and shrugged. "I guess we had better do it," I said. "But if they think I'm staying there for long, they're out of their minds. I'm going to wait until dark and sneak into the ward. I want to make sure the Troll is okay. She's like that because of us. Everyone on board with that?"

Eva nodded. Cairo didn't, but he looked away and didn't argue. A few minutes later, we were in my guest treehouse, where we waited. And waited. No one came to see us, or even question us. By the time the sun went down, I think we were all ready to get out of there.

I gathered us by the door and then as we left one-by-one, we each shifted into our dragons to get to the jungle floor, just in case the Elves could sense it when we "blipped" down. Then, we made our way to the medical ward. The Elves had grown it from the living trees themselves, like much of Paraiso, and it was just as beautiful.

Inside, through the openings where windows would be if it ever got cold in Paraiso, I saw three glowstones on each wall casting just enough light to see by. We had to wait a few minutes for the only person inside to leave, but then we were able to walk right in without even trying to hide.

I made my way to the Troll's bed and looked down at her. She was pale, and her breaths were quick and shallow. The sweat on her face shone in the glowstone light. Everything about her expression told me she was in agony. She looked like she was dying, and it was my fault.

I sat on the edge of the bed and put my hand on hers. The hair on my arm stood on end, moving like a wave from my hand all the way up to the back of my neck, and I shivered. I could almost feel her pain radiating out of her.

Her eyelids fluttered open, then. At first, she seemed to be staring right through me, but then I saw her eyes focus on mine. "Colton," she whispered.

I wanted her to speak up or tell me she was okay. I wanted her to get out of bed and get better. Instead, the effort from just saying my name seemed to make her shrink into herself, like it took away from whatever energy she had left in her.

"Yes, it's me. Tell me what I can do to help you, please," I whispered, and I felt my voice cracking. This was my fault.

"... closer ..."

I leaned down and put my ear near her face. "Tell me how to help, I'll do it," I said, more loudly than I should have.

"... the source ... in the land ... Fairies."

I shook my head and found myself clutching at her arm. "Forget the source, forget Fairies. How do we help you?" I cried out.

She didn't answer me, and even before I sat back upright, tears were streaming down my cheeks. The Troll would never cry again, which only made me cry harder.

Chapter Eleven

I blinked and looked at Eva helplessly. If even dragon and Elven healers couldn't do anything to save the Troll, what chance did I have? None.

Eva put her hand on my arm lightly. "It's not your fault, you know. I know you're going to blame yourself for this, but I'm telling you, don't. We had no way of knowing what would happen. Really, we don't actually know what *did* happen. But it had to have something to do with the reason Eldrick killed the Trolls and started the Earth to dying in the first place. This time, it was just one Troll. What if it had been a whole group? Now we can let them all know that the Trolls have to stay out of the black areas."

I shook my head, more to myself than to her. Of course, she would try to cheer me up, she was my friend, but no matter what she said, it was my fault. For this Troll, this time, she touched the black area because I asked her to. Maybe knowing it was deadly to them could save lives down the road, and maybe it would even give the big thinkers some new clue on how to solve all of this, but none of it made a difference to the poor Troll lying dead on the bed in the medical ward.

Cairo had been silent since the Troll died, so of course, he picked that moment to start talking again. "Eva is right. You probably saved lives. Plus, I'm thinking it might give the people back in Ochana something to think about. Maybe they can connect the dots in some new way and figure out what's going on."

I shouted, "No!" Then I tried to get myself under control. I took a breath and said, "Look, thanks for trying, but it's not going to make me feel better, and it's not going to bring her back, is it? She's dead, and no matter how you spin it, it's because I asked her to go into the black zone. Everything else is just what ifs and maybes, not facts. Not only that, she was the only Troll who would even talk to me, and now she's dead. Because of me. You think the others will want to talk to me after that? Yeah, probably not."

Eva frowned and scrunched her face, irritated. "Why do you care whether the Trolls like you or not? You're not a Troll, and that doesn't change our mission. Does it?"

"No, of course, it doesn't change our mission. But they don't like me, and I don't like that. What's it matter if it's important to the mission? It's important to me."

Cairo said, "If Jericho were here, he'd say—"

"Forget Jericho," I snapped, interrupting him. "He doesn't have any feelings in him to get hurt. He's a robot. Boo-hoo, his best friend died. A lot of people's best friends have died, and if this war keeps going, a lot more are going to lose best friends. He should get over it, but either way, I got my own problems to worry about, starting with an innocent Troll who died just for trying to help us."

Eva shook her head. "I know you're mad, but you aren't alone, and it isn't just happening to you. I'm here with you."

Of course, Eva was with me. She would have my back no matter what. I said, "Look, it's not that I don't appreciate that. I know we're all in this together. But she still died because I'm the Keeper of Dragons. I never asked for this, and I don't want it."

"What do you want?" Eva looked up at me and the concern in her eyes made me start to feel bad. Maybe I was being hard on her.

"Sometimes," I said with a heavy sigh, "I just wish I could go home. My real home, the people I grew up with. Not all of this." I waved my hand around, taking in Paraiso, Ochana, all of it.

The door opened and an Elf I didn't recognize stepped in. He wore the colors of Prince Gaber, though. When he saw us, he stopped suddenly and saluted. Then, standing as tall as he could and staring straight ahead, he said, "Prince Colton of Ochana. Prince Gaber and the Elven leaders request your immediate presence. I am here to escort you back at your soonest convenience."

It seemed pretty clear by his tone that he really meant right now, not whenever it was convenient. I clenched my fists and let out a frustrated huff through my nose. "It seems I'm being summoned. You're going to have to get along without me for a bit. Please see if we can do anything nice for that poor Troll, would you?"

Cairo snorted. "I'll give you one guess what Gaber and the other Elves want with you."

"Yeah," I said, staring at him, "it looks like they agree with me about who's responsible for all of this."

Before they had a chance to answer, I spun on my heels and stormed out the door, my Elf guardian rushing to catch up behind me. I kept going until we were out of sight, then I stopped and looked at him. "What am I walking into? I mean, how bad is it?"

"I'm not sure what you mean, Prince Colton."

"Please, just call me Cole. And I mean, how deep is the trouble I'm about to get in when I walk in that room?"

His face was blank. "That's not something they have told me... Cole. They just told me to bring you to them, but they didn't say why. It did sound rather urgent, though. Now, if you'd please come with me, they're waiting for you."

I held my hand out. "After you." Then, I fell into step beside him. We walked through Paraiso until we got to the Council room tree.

The escort saluted me. "Prince Gaber and his council await you. Good luck, Cole."

"Thanks."

I blinked up to the walkway, just outside the council chambers, then knocked hard three times on the door. I didn't want to seem timid and afraid at an important moment like that. If I was going to be in trouble for the poor Troll's death, I had to keep the situation under control so that it didn't cause any problems to affect the alliance. Without that, the Earth didn't stand a chance. I didn't know if it stood a chance even with the alliance.

The door swung open on its own, startling me a little bit. I gathered myself up and straightened my shirt, then marched inside. Prince Gaber and his sister were there, along with three other Elves. I had seen the other three around Paraiso and knew they were important, but I didn't know who they were.

I looked at Gaber directly and said, "You asked for me to come see you. I'm here, of course. How can I help you?"

"Yes, thank you for coming. I'm sure you know why we've called you. The death of a Troll after touching one of the black spots. It has all the Elves and Trolls frightened. The black areas have been expanding unpredictably, and new spots are still appearing. We haven't figured out any pattern as to how or when they will appear. It means that one could very well pop up right here in the middle of Paraiso. If Elves and Trolls die the instant they touch the black spots, I'm sure you can see why they're afraid."

When Gaber mentioned the Troll who had died, I could see the blame in his eyes. It matched the guilt I felt. He stared at me, but I couldn't meet his eyes. Instead, I glanced from Elf to Elf, trying to look stronger than I felt. I said, "Yes, I get it. I understand why they're afraid, and they should be. We don't know why it killed the Troll when she touched it. I've touched it and it didn't harm me."

Gaber gritted his teeth. "I hope you see now how reckless that was. What if it had killed the Keeper of Dragons?"

"Then a black spot would have done what King Eldrick couldn't," I snapped.

Gaber shouted, "Don't you mention his name here!" He took a deep breath, trying to calm himself. He said, "My brother is a traitor, not a king. And touching the black spot was reckless."

"I know," I replied, "and I had no idea what it was, but I touched it anyway. Worse, I sent someone else to go do the same, but I didn't know it would kill her."

"That's right, you didn't know. You cost a good Troll her life. I knew her, Cole, and I'm not the only one who will miss her."

I looked down at the floor. I just couldn't look him in the eyes. "I know. Because I was fine when I touched it, I assumed everyone else would be, too."

One of the other Elves said loudly, "Aha! So, the dragon admits he is at fault."

My head snapped around to face him and I hissed, "Don't twist my words. My fault? Did I plunge a dagger into her chest like your king's brother did? No. I asked her to do something I had already done myself. I don't ask people to do things I wouldn't do. Can you say the same?"

Oh, no. Too late, I realized what I'd done. He had just made me so angry by blaming me for the Troll's death as if I was the killer. Eldrick did it, not me. In the middle of the stunned silence, I said, "I'm sorry. That was disrespectful of me, and I apologize. I know that everyone is tense, and we're all upset over her death. She seemed like a good person, even though I barely knew her. I feel her death like a heavy weight. The truth is, I blame myself just as much as you do."

The Elf opened his mouth and leaned forward, gripping the arms of his chair, eyes shining like he finally had me where he wanted me, but Prince Gaber cut him off, slamming his fist down on the arm of his chair.

"Silence! Cole, taking responsibility for what you did surprises me. I have not come to expect that from dragons. I have one question. Why did you ask her to touch it? What did you hope to get out of that?"

Well, they couldn't judge me any harder than I was already judging myself, so I shoved my irritation aside. It didn't really matter what happened to me, anyway. The only thing that really mattered was the war, the Time of Fear. It's not like Gaber would let them execute me. I didn't think they could, even if they wanted to.

But, if I wanted to beat Eldrick and push back the blackness, I needed a strong alliance. If that meant apologizing to a scared and angry elf who snapped at me, I could handle that. I said, "We were hoping that she might discover something about the spots that we'd missed. Maybe she could smell something, or maybe the black spots had something to do with Trolls. I mean, we know it had something to do with them in the beginning, when…"

"When my brother killed so many of them."

"Yes. I thought maybe there would be a connection between the Troll and the spot, and we might be able to learn something and we could use it against it."

"I see how you might think that." Gaber shot a hard glance at the Elf I'd insulted, like a warning to be silent. I think they were talking telepathically, but I wasn't part of the conversation, so I couldn't be sure. "And what did her death teach you? Did you learn anything that you might use against Eldrick and his spots?"

I took a deep breath and let it out slowly. "No. We didn't learn anything from her death. It was just one more pointless murder by your brother and his forces. But there's more we *have* learned."

Gaber shook his head. His eyes were narrowed, looking at me. "You make no sense. What do you mean that you didn't learn anything, but you did? Explain yourself."

So, I told him and his Elves all about what I'd done—seeing the light, talking to Ancestors, pumping every ounce of energy I could into the bush and bringing it back to life.

They sat silently, and the expressions on their faces told me they were as surprised as I had been. That was a relief because I'd have lost my mind if I thought they knew something like that and kept it from me just because I was a dragon. The only thing I'd left out was the ring. I kept that to just me and Eva, and her only because she'd been there to see it. It was our secret. I don't know why, but it felt important to keep it private between us.

At first, they weren't fully convinced about bringing the bush back to life, but when they had a black leaf brought in by a glove-wearing Elf, I closed my eyes and did my thing, and when I opened them, the leaf was green again. They were shocked and stared at it a long time.

Then I said, "And my Troll friend said one last thing before she went to her Ancestors. She said, 'The source is in the land of the Fairies.'"

Gaber stood up and started to pace in front of his chair, walking back and forth with his hands behind his back, looking at the floor. Then he stopped mid-step and looked up at me. "Then it's settled. Although the Troll's death is on your hands, I think you feel remorse, and I am pretty sure you'll use your head before you risk someone else's life on a whim the next time."

"Yes, I—"

"It wasn't a question. One more thing is settled, too—you have to go to the Fairy realm. Maybe we should have sent you there in the beginning, I don't know. The Fates don't ask me how things should happen."

I said, "I'm sure you don't mind the fact that it takes me away from Paraiso."

He ignored the comment. "Find the source of this cancer in the Earth, and cure it. Only you can stop the land from dying, Prince Colton."

It was the first time I felt like he'd said my name without a sneer in his voice since I'd met him. I could almost feel his desperate hope sitting on my shoulders, and I didn't like it. I'd have rather had him sneering at me than inspiring unrealistic hope. What could I really do? Heal one spot. Not exactly legendary.

But I'd wanted to go to the Fairies in the beginning, before we went to the Mermaids. If I had, I wouldn't have learned to use mereum, and I wouldn't have been able to turn the black green again. So maybe Fate had planned that part out, and maybe it still had some new surprises in store for me among the Fairies. There was only one way to find out.

Chapter Twelve

"I'll go." I tried to stand tall, looking confident. I didn't really feel it, but they didn't have to know that.

You can do it, though. Eva's voice was in my head. I hoped she was the only one listening in.

Gaber gave me a quick nod. "Then it's settled. But be aware that after what happened with the Troll, you aren't welcome back in Paraiso. You're just too dangerous to have around. Besides, your quest is out there, not tucked safely here with us. When you've cured it so the blackness no longer threatens the world, then you'll be welcome back with open arms."

I was stunned. Exiled from Paraiso! I loved Paraiso's jungle paradise. I understood the decision, but I felt like part of me had been cut off. If I wanted it back, I had to save it first. "I understand. I won't let you down. As long as I'm still breathing, I'll be out there fighting for you and all the other races of Truth."

Hey, it sounded good in my head, even if it came out a little melodramatic.

Gaber nodded, then raised a small wooden staff from where it leaned against his chair and banged the metal-tipped bottom against the floor three times. It made an impressive booming noise. It also made it clear I was dismissed, so I turned and left without another word.

Outside, Cairo and Eva waited for me. She was the first to speak up when they saw me. "How did it go? Are you in trouble?" She looked really worried, biting her bottom lip.

"It wasn't great. They blame me for the Troll dying. They think I'm too dangerous to have around. So, I'm being kicked out."

"What! They—"

"They'll let me back in when we fix the planet. No biggie."

Cairo's eyes went wide as his cheeks turned red. "That's not fair! How were you to know what would happen? Let me go in there and tell them—"

"No," I said, cutting him off. I put my hand on his shoulder and looked right into his eyes. "Thank you for standing up for me. But they're right. My place is out there fighting Eldrick, not hiding here, where it's safe. That's an illusion anyway, because not even Paraiso will stay safe. Not if I don't fix this."

Eva slid her arm around my waist and nudged my shoulder with her cheek. "You mean until we fix this. I'm in. Where are we going?"

"Me too," Cairo said. "I go where Eva goes, but I'd come with you anyway. We're in it together, right?"

A voice behind me made me jump. "You weren't going to leave without me, were you?"

I spun around, startled, and saw Jericho. "You're back! Where did you go?"

"I had some things to look into, and some people I had to question."

"And did you learn anything?"

"I didn't find out anything new, unfortunately. Give it time. We'll see where it leads. I won't say more until I have something worth sharing with the Keepers," Jericho said with a nod to Eva, his eyes still on me. "Where are we going, and when do we leave?"

"I was just getting to that," I said, grinning. "I'll be a lot happier with you coming with us. We need to head to the land of the Fairies. We only have one clue, and it says we'll find the source in Greece."

Eva pulled her arm out from around my waist. She stepped up beside Cairo and looked up at Jericho. "Well, you get your wish after all, Cole. Maybe we should have gone there first."

I laughed since I'd had the same thought. "No, you were right. Fate works however it wants to. If we hadn't gone to see the Mermaid queen first, I wouldn't have learned how to turn the blackness green again."

Jericho let out a bark. His eyes flared brightly as he said, "You can fix this? How? Tell me everything."

I tried not to laugh at his reaction. "It turns out that if I focus mahier, tilium, and mereum at something, it comes back to life and the black goes away. I don't know how long it lasts, and I sure can't do it faster than all the black spots grow, but it's a start."

Jericho clapped me on my shoulder hard enough to sting, grinning. "You can say that again. That's one fine start, Cole. I would never have even thought to try, but then again, you're the only one of us who has more than one power. Aprella is smiling on us."

I grinned right back, but said, "Don't sing my praises, yet. We have to get to Greece and talk to the Fairies. I'm not sure what 'the source is in the land of the Fairies' means, but we'll find out when we get there."

"A wing of dragons will follow us and meet us there," he said. "Now, everyone, go grab your stuff and meet me back here in fifteen minutes. Actually, make that a half-hour so we can eat before we leave. I'm hungrier than I realized."

So was I, actually. I left the group and got me a fat cow to eat, then went and got my backpack.

The others were already at the clearing by the time I got there. Cairo said, "What kept you, slowpoke? I'm ready when you are."

I gave him a thumbs-up, then turned and leaped into the air, shifting into my dragon. They were right behind me, and the four of us rose up and away, leaving beautiful Paraiso behind. I hoped I would get to see it again, someday.

As we rose high above the Congo jungles, I could see for miles. The blackness had spread, that was for sure. It seemed like there was more black than green now, wherever I looked. It made me sad to think of all the poor animals and plants that were dying.

I sped up. The miles streaked by, and I let myself zone out. It was nice to just let everything fade away and focus on the feel of the wind on my face, the way the clouds tickled my wings when we flew through them. We flew like that, hour after hour.

When the sun began to sink into the horizon, I felt Jericho's thoughts in my mind. *We need to stop for the night. I know a dragon living in this area who will take us in. Follow me down, and I'll introduce you to him. Then we can get something to eat.*

I tipped my wings to let him know I heard him, then banked slowly to the west, following him down at a lazy speed. I wished he'd hurry up since I was practically starving, but I thought he might have a reason for going so slow. Maybe the dragon we were seeing wouldn't like a bunch of us streaking down from the sky at almost the speed of sound.

We landed in a rocky clearing surrounded by a big stretch of palm trees. That meant we were still in Africa, I figured, which kind of surprised me. We had been flying pretty fast. Then I remembered how I lost track of time daydreaming.

Anyway, I shifted into my human as we landed, then turned to Jericho. "Where is your friend? I don't see any houses, here."

He started walking toward the tree line. "He lives in a hut in the palm tree forest. There's a trail to his hut, but unless you know it's there, he has hidden it with his mahier."

We followed Jericho and he headed directly toward a tree. I thought he would go around it, but he didn't even slow down. He walked right through it! That must be the trail, I realized—and then it appeared to me. Trees shimmered away, revealing a nice trail that had been well-maintained. Somebody took the time to clear away all the weeds and underbrush regularly, too.

We must have walked for half an hour because it had become nearly dark. Jericho pointed up ahead, and I turned to look. I had to squint to see it, but there was a log house in the distance. Calling it a hut wasn't really fair, because it looked big. It was only one story high, but even from our distance, I could tell it had room for several bedrooms. I had been picturing a little hunting cabin, not a full-sized log house.

When we got about a few hundred feet away, Jericho stopped and held up his hand. "I think you should wait here. He doesn't know you, and he's out here because he wants his privacy. I'll go talk to him and then I'll come get you."

Eva and Cairo nodded, but for some reason, the hairs on the back of my neck stood up and I felt goosebumps down my arms, despite the heat. "No, I don't think that's a good idea. You've seen how Eldrick's people have been following us. If we separate, it's just that much easier to catch us. I think we should stay together, especially with the blackness so close."

Jericho said, "There's blackness everywhere you go. I'll be fine. Just wait here."

"Say what you want, but I'm coming with you unless you want to stop me."

A little puff of smoke drifted from his nostrils, but he didn't say anything. He spun on his heels and stormed toward the hut. I had to scramble to catch up.

As we got closer, we found a small, rock-lined path up to the house itself. Jericho didn't slow down until we were almost to the front patio.

"Is it normal for him to have all the lights out?" I asked, "I mean, it's dark already. Maybe he's asleep."

Jericho stopped mid-stride and I almost walked right into him. He held his arm out to keep me back. "No. If he's home, there should be lights on, and he's always home. I hope he's okay. We need to check it out. Stay close and keep your eyes open."

We headed to the house, my eyes darting everywhere, trying to see everything at once. When we got to the patio, what we found only made me more nervous. He had beautiful, hand-carved chairs and a table on his patio, but they had been tossed around. One of the chairs was smashed into pieces. The door wasn't closed all the way, either, and hung from its top hinge.

I whispered, "Let's check inside. He might be hurt."

Jericho shook his head and pushed me back away from the house. "No, I've seen enough. We need to get out of here. Someone knew we were coming and may still be in the area. It could be a trap. I'm sad to say it but the Keeper of Dragons matters a lot more than my friend, or even me, right now. Move out, Cole."

I didn't argue. I'd had enough close calls with Eldrick's people to know how bad things could get and how fast they could get there. We hurried back to where Eva and Cairo stood waiting for us.

I said, "He's not home. This could be a trap, so get to the air."

Without waiting for a response, I turned and jumped into the air, summoning my dragon. I poured as much mahier as I could into disguising us and hiding our presence, hoping not to be seen by anyone on the ground.

The others followed, and I could feel their mahier pouring over me as well, making the disguise even stronger. They'd had the same idea.

I projected my thoughts at Jericho. "How would they have known we were coming here? That had to happen recently, right? Otherwise, your friend's illusion would be gone already."

I heard Jericho's deep, rumbly voice in my mind saying, "You're right. I don't know who knew we were coming or how. It's something we should definitely be worried about. Maybe a spy, or maybe they're tracking us again. I guess we're flying through the night, Keeper."

After an hour, Africa's coastline gave way to the Mediterranean Sea. At night, it looked like a giant hole of inky blackness, much like the black spots, but I knew it was just an illusion. There weren't any cities in the ocean, after all, so no light at all. We didn't even slow down to eat before we flew out to sea.

We must've been about halfway to Europe when I noticed the wind picking up. At first, I just thought it was the ocean breeze, but I kept having to put more mahier into keeping the wind from bothering us. When I had to concentrate even harder, I thought out to Jericho, "What's wrong with the wind? Are we in a storm?"

I didn't understand how it could be a storm, though, because there weren't any clouds. The stars all sparkled brightly above us. And I hadn't felt the wind like that since I learned to keep it off me while flying. We were going way faster than a hurricane.

"Not any storm I can see," his voice echoed in my mind. "I feel it, too."

Something was terribly wrong.

Chapter Thirteen

A burst of wind slipped through my mahier screen and blew me sideways, sending me almost crashing into Cairo. He dodged out of the way at the last moment, but then he caught a gust of wind as he lifted his wings to turn away. It carried him like a kite, up and away, sending him a hundred yards in an instant.

We struggled to get back together and keep formation. Being close together made it easier for us all to pour our mahier into shielding the whole group, layering our powers on top of each other for more protection, but my wings were getting tired from the struggle. When we got hit by another windy hammer, fear radiated from Eva, slipping through her mental screen as she focused everything on her windscreen instead.

She wasn't the only one afraid. I was having a hard time keeping my thoughts to myself, too. I think we all were, and that storm or whatever it was seemed to still be getting worse. We tried to keep together, but I think we spent more of our energy doing that than we did moving forward, toward land.

Then the clouds appeared, but not just any old normal clouds. They didn't just blow in with the storm. At first, they rose up like a thick fog, but soon, we had ugly, black rolling clouds everywhere around us.

Lightning flashed deep inside the clouds, the thunder booming like some terrifying war drums. Every time it flashed, it turned the wicked black clouds red. They looked like fire and anger. I don't know how I knew it, but I felt like those clouds were hunting us.

It was no natural storm! I could *feel* dark tilium practically oozing from the clouds, I suddenly realized.

The lighting had been distant, deep inside the clouds around us, but just when I realized they were dark tilium, they burst into the biggest, scariest display I'd ever seen. Half a dozen bolts shot from the clouds, one bigger than any I'd seen before. Each bolt forked ten, then twenty times, and even more! When they all flashed at once, the huge storm lit up like a candle in a paper bag, and I could have sworn I saw Eldrick's face coming through. A face of red fire-clouds and lightning. An angry, insane face...

The bolts started to get closer and closer, moving toward us. At the same time, we got hit by even stronger hammer winds, swatting us down like bugs. The blows came at us from above, and I think I lost a thousand feet of altitude in seconds. The lightning was herding us, keeping us from going back up—we couldn't fly above the storm if we couldn't survive the trip up there.

"We have to land!" I shouted my thoughts to the others. My fear and tilium worked together like a bullhorn, making my thoughts stronger and louder.

I couldn't hear their answers over the noise of the storm and my own projected thoughts, echoing in my mind. I could only feel their agreement and their fear.

We didn't have much choice, though, because the hammering winds pushed us down and down, throwing us at the water below. What a way to end.

"Lights," Jericho's voice came into my mind from the darkness, but he sounded far away. I didn't see, him but I looked down and saw a town lit up. He was right. It was land!

I swept my wings back and fell like a dart, dropping away from the lightning and wind. I aimed for a spot just outside the glow from the town lights. Just before I hit the ground, I stretched out my wings and tilted them back. The sudden resistance brought me to a stop so fast my teeth clicked together so hard that I thought they might break.

I dropped the last ten feet to the ground, summoning my human as I landed, and fell to my knees. I didn't think anything broke, though, so I struggled to my feet, calling for the others as loudly as I could. I didn't hear any reply, even in my head. I tried again, but there was nothing. They were gone.

I heard a faint cry high above me. I looked up and saw wings flying my way, pumping against the terrible wind. I couldn't tell who it was until I heard the voice in my head again. It was Eva!

"Cole, I'm coming!" she cried.

A bolt of lightning came at her with a flash and a roar. Instinctively, I flung my hand out toward her. I felt mereum stronger than I'd ever used before, making a shield around her. The lightning hit it and was knocked aside! The shield cracked into a thousand shards of mereum, which dissolved back into the storm as they dropped.

A moment later, I was catching Eva as she crash-landed in human form, and we fell to the ground together, hard. It knocked the wind out of me but probably saved her from getting hurt from her fall. We lay there for a moment, gasping for air and praying not to get hit by lightning.

I didn't have to worry, though. As soon as she touched down, the storm lightened and then faded away to nothing in a matter of just moments. The tilium I'd felt everywhere was gone, my senses told me. Eldrick was gone.

"Are you okay?" I asked Eva.

She slowly untangled herself from me and climbed to her feet, then helped me up. "Yeah. Bruised, but not broken. Do you feel the others close by?"

I frowned. "I'd hoped you did. No, I can't feel either of them, and I know there was a Woland realm flying after us. I don't feel them, either."

She was silent, lips pursed. I understood the feeling perfectly well.

I said, "They must have been blown somewhere else. We could fly around looking for them. It seems the storm faded as soon as we landed, so you must have been the last to touch down."

She turned suddenly to face me and narrowed her eyes as she shouted, "No! Until we know for sure it's safe, we're walking. And we can't waste time looking for them, not when we have a mission to finish. Where would you even look?"

I took a step back, surprised by how fierce she was about it. "Fine, okay. No flying. We'll walk. I don't know where we'd look. I just thought you would want to. Cairo—"

"—knows where we're headed! You need to use your head more, Cole. We could spend months trying to find them, only to learn they did the smart thing and went to the Fairies. Just like we should be doing."

She stared at me for a few seconds, and then I saw the tension leave her shoulders and her eyes stopped being all squinty at me. "Sorry. That storm was terrifying, and I'm scared for the others, too. But we can't spend time looking for them. If they're alive, they know where we're going. They'll head there."

I stepped up and wrapped my arms around her. I thought maybe it would help her because I knew she wasn't saying everything. She had to be nearly panicked about Cairo, after all. She struggled for a second, then just let me hug her. Finally, she hugged me back.

After a moment, she stepped back, wiped her cheeks with the heels of her hands, and sniffled. "Fine, you big goof. Ick, feelings. Can we go now, please?"

I grinned at her and then turned north. "I figure we're in Greece," I said over my shoulder. "Fairies are here somewhere, right?"

"Yeah." She rushed to catch up, then settled into step next to me. "The grove ought to be a few miles that way." She pointed northeast.

It only took a half an hour of walking to find the grove. It wasn't as big as the Congo jungle, of course, but it was still pretty big. I could tell from the tilium in it that it would look like something else to a normal human, shielded like Paraiso was.

I felt my heartbeat rising in excitement at the thought of seeing our friends again soon and picked up my pace. Eva was grinning as we entered the grove.

"Fairies! Eva, can you feel it?" She was about to say something in reply when her eyes went suddenly wide, looking at me. I felt something cold, hard, and sharp against my throat. "What the...?"

"Silence, dragons," a high-pitched voice said from behind me. Another figure stepped out from behind a tree next to Eva. Well, it looked like it stepped out from *inside* the tree. Either way, Eva got a knife held to her throat, too.

My stomach sank. Fantastic. Held at knife-point by Fairies, the very people we'd come to see. What had I done this time?

Chapter Fourteen

"Get your hands off her! How dare you? We're the Keep—"

The fairy holding me at knifepoint yanked my hair, dragging my head back. "The Keeper of Dragons. Yeah, we know who you are," he hissed into my ear. "And you'll get what's coming to you, too. Come quietly and get it a few minutes later, or struggle and you'll get it now."

Eva cried out, "No! We'll come. I swear, no fighting. Cole, stay calm."

I wasn't trying to freak out, not with a knife digging into my neck. "We'll come, take it easy. I have no idea what you mean, but—"

"Shut up!" My Fairy swung me around to face down the path. "Walk," he commanded.

I glanced at Eva and started walking. If we could just stay alive long enough to talk to someone in charge, I knew this could all be cleared up. I wasn't sure what the misunderstanding was, but I was totally certain that our lives depended on us finding out and fixing it.

The Fairies dragged us deeper into the grove. After a few minutes, I saw buildings ahead, and my heart beat faster. The Fairy realm, at last! But as we got closer, my excitement turned sour.

The destruction I saw there was enough to make me want to cry. Every building was smashed or burned; every garden was black with many still smoking, just as many of the homes still did. The windows everywhere had been stained glass, and I could just imagine how beautiful it must have been there with daylight streaming through a thousand colored windows. But no more. The windows had been smashed and destroyed, just like the village itself.

My jaw dropped. I looked at the Fairy holding me prisoner and saw tears welling up in his eyes, and his jaw was clenched so tightly that the muscles stood out on his cheeks. "What happened?" I asked.

The Fairies didn't answer me. They just kept dragging and prodding Eva and me to keep moving.

We came around a corner in the road and saw the main village square. It was wrecked, too, and lots of people were wearing bandages. Eldrick would pay for what he'd done here. I promised that much.

I saw people on their knees in the middle of the village square and realized it was Jericho and Cairo. Some of the missing Woland Realm that had followed us into the storm was there also. They were alive! But many were missing. They all had their wrists tied in front of them, and my mahier told me the ropes were enchanted. I guessed it was to keep Jericho and the others from summoning their dragon forms.

"What on Earth is going on?" I asked, trying again. My kidnapper still didn't answer.

When we got close to Jericho, Eva and I were shoved down to the dirt next to him. All around, armed Fairies stood guard over us, staring with angry eyes. I was pretty sure someone had ordered them not to hurt us because they looked like they would have enjoyed running us through with their swords and spears.

Jericho's eye was swelling shut. Someone had kicked him in the face, I could tell because the bruise was shoe-shaped. He saw me looking at his swollen eye and shrugged.

I tried to keep my voice low enough for him to hear it, but not loud enough for the Fairies to, and asked him, "Do you know what happened here?"

It didn't work. One of the guards shouted, "Shut your mouth, *Dragon*." The way he said it was like dragon was a bad word or something.

"Actually," a woman behind me said, "let's hear what these monsters have to say before we give them the justice they deserve. We're civilized, here, unlike you people. We let defendants have their say first, and *then* we execute them."

I craned my neck to see her. I didn't recognize her. She carried herself with perfect posture, though, like someone used to being in charge. She had elegant features but the effect was ruined by the red-stained bandage wrapped around her head.

Then what she'd said registered in my head. "Wait. Execute us?" My eyes popped and I shouted, "On what charges?"

One of the guards behind me kicked me in the back, knocking me down. "Mind your tone."

The woman sneered at us while I got back up to my knees. "Do you really want to go through with this game? Fine, we'll pretend you don't know."

Through her clenched jaw, Eva said, "We don't know. There's no pretending. So maybe you could humor us with an explanation before you murder us."

The Fairy leader rolled her eyes. "Fine. You stand charged with being dragons, the same fiends who attacked this sacred place—our *home*—destroying it and killing our people. When we beg for mercy, you ignore our pleas, but you want us to show you the mercy you denied us?

"That wasn't us, it was—"

"You dragons have become mad beasts! No one can reason with you. You're destroying everything around you. Where was the mercy you ask for when you were attacking us?" She'd gone from talking with ice in her voice to shouting, full of fiery anger.

I was stunned as I heard myself shouting back, before I realized what I was doing, "Impossible!

Maybe dragons don't get along with most other races, but we aren't killers. We don't attack another True being for no reason."

There were about two seconds of total silence as everyone stared at me, shocked. I crossed my arms over my chest and added, "I never heard any such thing from my father, or from anyone in Ochana. Never."

The woman's eyes flashed. "Liar!"

Jericho spoke for the first time. "Prince Colton is no liar, Fairy, and he's the only one who can heal your grove."

Her eyes flicked over to look at me. "Heal it? And yet, here we are, having captured the dragon prince himself after he came to our grove to spread more chaos. Proof that you dragons are working against us now. What do you have to say to that, boy?"

The guard who had kicked me said from behind me, "Speak quickly, while you still can."

I only had one shot. I had to make it good. The fairies were scared, hurt, and angry, and they weren't looking for reasons to talk things out.

"Dragons like me use the power, mahier. Some of you know how I also can use purified tilium."

The guard said, "That's nothing new. You're stalling."

"No! What you don't know is that I use mereum, too. When I use all three powers together, I can bring your grove back. It even works on the blackness spreading everywhere."

I was kind of proud of all that but tried not to sound like it. I kept my eyes looking down at the ground and hoped I didn't seem like I was bragging.

"The blackness! You dragons brought that, so of course, you're the only ones who can fix it. You destroyed our grove, and you turned the rest out to rot. You only left us our village, and now you've destroyed that, too." She looked like she might burst into tears, but I saw steel in her eyes.

"None of us here did that, but I really can fix it. The blackness is everywhere, not just here. If you left your realm to help the rest of the world, you'd know this. Eldrick created the blackness when he killed the Trolls."

The village leader stopped and stared at me, and I felt like she was trying to see into my aura for lies. She probably was, but must not have found what she expected, because then she let out a long, frustrated sigh. "The Trolls are gone?" she asked at last.

Eva blurted, "Many of them. Where their blood hit the ground, the black spots started. He killed them all over the world, and the dark spots are growing on their own. The Trolls that Cole and I rescued"—she nodded to indicate me—"are taking refuge with the Elves in Paraiso."

I saw the guards look at their leader. They looked tense and ready. This was it, the moment of truth. They'd either buy it, or they'd be playing "stabby-stabby cut-cut" with us really soon.

"Very well, if the Keeper can heal our grove, then I'll know you're telling us the truth. We'll go from there. But if you've lied, killing you won't bring our grove back, but it'll be some small justice."

I got to my feet and squared my shoulders. I looked her in the eyes and said, "Then we should get started. Where do you want me to begin?"

Chapter Fifteen

As the Fairies led me to the center of their grove, I kept stumbling from the chains and shackles they'd put us all in. It also made it hard to catch my balance, and I probably got more than a few bruises from falling down along the way. Each time I fell, Fairy guards helped me to my feet. Some were gentle, some were rough. It was obvious that I hadn't convinced them all, not yet.

But that's what we're on our way to do, right?

I glanced over at Eva and gave her a quick nod, but before I could think back at her, my foot caught on a root and I fell face-first into the blackened, dead soil. I let out a sharp, frustrated breath. We'd been walking longer than I thought we should have, but the growth seemed larger on the inside than it had looked when we were flying in. The chains might have been slowing me down, but it still felt like we should have reached the center faster. Eventually, though, we got there more or less in one piece.

The Fairy Queen was already there, waiting for us. After she'd been told what happened, the chains had been her idea, despite everything we went through together in Paraiso. The chains weren't the only thing frustrating me. The fact that she believed the nonsense about dragons attacking them showed me just how low people's opinions of Ochana had gone during my grandfather's reign as king.

She said, "We are in the heart of our sacred Grove. You swore to heal the land, and so I am giving you the chance to do so. You are in the enviable position of holding your fate in your own hands. Most people don't get that chance. Certainly, the Trolls didn't. I wish you luck, Prince Colton."

I turned to face her, then gave her a deep bow. She looked surprised, but it didn't hurt anything for me to show her respect in her realm, after all. I knew I could cure the blackness, so I figured I would score some brownie points at the same time. "I need the chains off my wrists, Queen. I have to have clear flow for my energies to work right."

When she narrowed her eyes, I hastily added, "But you can leave the ankle cuffs on, of course. It's just my hands."

She motioned to one of the guards and nodded. He came over and unlocked both cuffs.

I rubbed my wrists, grimacing as the blood flowed back into my hands, setting them to pins and needles. Then I took a few long, slow breaths and focused my will. I channeled my mahier and tilium through my hands, down into the soil, while I drew mereum from the air and guided that into the soil, too.

With my eyes still closed, I heard gasps of surprise all around me. I cracked one eyelid open enough to glance around; the queen had both hands over her mouth and stared at her trees with eyes as wide as saucers.

I tried not to grin and focused on keeping the energy pouring into the grove. I could *feel* the life returning, and as the plants and insects came back, I felt the grove's deep tilium pool coming back, too. Bigger and bigger, the circle of life grew all around us. Some of the Fairies even started laughing with joy to see their home returning to them.

I wasn't sure how long I'd been working at it, but eventually, I felt the very last of the blackness vanish—in this place, at least, the curse upon the Earth was completely gone.

The queen put one hand on my shoulder, looking me in the eyes, and smiled. "Prince Colton—Cole, as you like to be called—you have kept your word. You and your friends are free, and I name you Friends of the Grove. Will you stay for a banquet tonight? We need to celebrate the return of our grove! It would mean a lot to me if you would join us."

Before Eva could blurt out something to ruin the moment, I agreed. Besides, I was really hungry after the flight we'd had.

***

That night, just as the brightest stars began shining up above, my friends and I were led to the Fairies' Great Hall. I saw barrels and barrels of wine and ale open, but I wasn't interested in those things.

After using so much energy earlier, the only thing I had eyes for was the huge feast that filled up a dozen long tables laid out end-to-end. I had never seen so much food in one place. My mouth watered.

Nearby, costumed Fairies played music on instruments that glittered every time the strings were plucked or a key was pressed. They played strange music, but it was beautiful. Whatever they played, there were always four main chords but if I strained hard enough to listen, I could almost hear a fifth note. It was like the four tones together made a new one.

At the head of the table stood the queen. When she spoke, her voice reached every corner of the hall though she seemed to be talking in a normal voice, not shouting. "My people, we have our grove back. Eldrick tried to take it from us, not the dragons, but it was the dragons who gave it back. It may be the last thing we expected, I know, but the truth is easy to see all around us. Our power returned with it, and so tonight, we celebrate! Let's rejoice in our home and our new friends. "

The Fairies all around clapped, so I did, too. I was led to a seat close to the head of the table, while my companions were seated farther away, but still close enough to the queen to be in places of honor. Fairies were masters at politics, it seemed. I raised a cup of cider to the queen, and she smiled and raised hers to me.

I didn't care where they sat me, just as long as I could get to all that beautiful, beautiful food. There were meat and fish, both roasted and fried. Mushrooms sautéed with shallots. Every kind of plant, even many I couldn't recognize, baked, fried, raw, or pickled. Basically, they had food in every delicious way there was to eat it. Okay, I wasn't sure about the pickled stuff, but I wasn't going to complain. I'd never been to a Fairy banquet before, and Jericho had told me that very few outsiders were ever invited.

As the party went on into the night, after I'd eaten all I wanted to and more, I was having a great time. Even Jericho didn't bug me as much as usual. I hadn't realized how badly I needed to set aside all the danger and fear and drama going on in the world, even if I knew it would only be for a night.

As it turned out, my vacation from all of that didn't last very long.

The Crowns' Accord

Chapter Sixteen

I was about to dig into another helping of some weird-looking but deliciously roasted bird when a horn sounded outside, and then another horn blew even closer. The queen jumped to her feet and cried, "To arms! We're under attack."

I rushed outside, drawing my sword, and found Jericho at my side. A nearby building was burning, its walls smashed by a big red dragon, who still stood in front of it. When he turned to look at me, I almost panicked--the thing reminded me of a wild beast. He had crazy, red eyes and smoke poured from his nostrils. He snarled and drew a deep breath, getting ready to unload fire again.

"Get the queen back!" I shouted to Jericho, then sprinted at the rampaging dragon. How dare he stoop so low as to work with Eldrick! I wanted nothing more than to punish that traitor. When I got close, I drew my sword. I wasn't going to let him harm our allies.

The dragon ignored me and blew a cone of fire at Jericho, who was leading the queen away, but Jericho threw up a mahier shield and the flame parted harmlessly around them. "I know him!" he shouted to me. "He's an old soldier."

Something wasn't right, I just had a strong feeling about it. I couldn't put my finger on what it was, though. I stopped myself from skewering him with my sword, and instead, jumped over the dragon's lashing tail. I shouted back to Jericho, "When did he turn traitor?"

He raised his hands over his head, then brought them both down in the dragon's direction; faintly glimmering mahier threads as thick as ropes appeared and draped themselves over our attacker. "He didn't turn traitor! He was too rational for that. I saw him last week—"

He was interrupted when the dragon flexed his heavy wings, shattering the ropes, and the back-blast channeled back to knock Jericho to his knees.

"Let's see how you deal with something new," I muttered. I imagined new cords over the dragon, willing them to appear, and wove them together by moving my hands over each other. This time, though, they were made of tilium, not mahier.

Eva and Cairo arrived and flanked the dragon so one stood on both sides of him. I saw them throwing more mahier bonds over the creature. I was glad they figured out what Jericho and I were trying to do because I didn't want to kill the thing. You can't question a dead dragon, after all.

Jericho scrambled back to his feet and, raising both fists over his head and then swinging his arms down to his sides, he placed a mahier dome over the dragon, adding to the threads.

It thrashed and roared and growled, but never once used words. The only thoughts I got from it weren't in words either, but more like picture-thoughts. Lots of angry red hues. The more it thrashed, the harder we all concentrated on keeping it bound.

"Ropes!" I yelled. "Get this thing tied up. I'm using tilium like crazy, but it isn't slowing down."

That was strange, but the creature really didn't seem to be getting tired at all, no matter how hard or how long it fought. I realized we were getting tired faster than it was, even with five of us. It would have been a lot easier to just kill him, but we needed information.

Thankfully, no one else got hurt while our crew of dragons—Jericho, Eva, Cairo, and I—all fought to get the invading dragon tied up with real ropes. When that was done, I put my hands on my knees, and sweating, and let my tilium cords fade away.

The queen walked up to me, but her eyes never left the tied-up dragon. She said, "Why didn't you kill it?" It sounded more like an accusation than a question.

I stood as tall and straight as I could when I replied, just out of respect, though I still hadn't caught my breath. "Something's wrong... It's not... acting right. We need to... question the thing."

She nodded but looked relieved. Maybe she'd thought we were just being nice because it was a dragon like us. That was a little bit true, I suppose, but it wasn't the main reason we'd tied him up instead of killing him.

Jericho said, "You made a good choice not to kill him, Cole. I knew that man, and he was a very sensible person, a methodical warrior, not some crazy berserker. He shouldn't be acting like this. And did you notice, when you try to talk to him, it's like he's not listening?"

"Yeah. And the thoughts I read from him were in pictures, not words," I replied. "A lot like how I think animals would do it."

Eva tapped her lips with one finger while she looked over at our new prisoner. He was still trying to fight his way loose, though he could hardly move an inch with all the chains and ropes we had tied him up with. "We need to study him. Somewhere with labs and doctors, I think. We—"

Trumpets blared from above, cutting her off. I looked up and saw two dragons, a man and a woman dragon judging by their sizes, with banners of Second Realm, Ochana's recon force. They spiraled down toward us, slowing a bit with each circle, but they were moving faster than they should be as they rushed to land. When they touched down and summoned their human forms, they staggered from the speed, but neither one fell. They both bowed to Queen Annabelle, then knelt in front of me with their left hand over their chest, saluting.

The man said, "My prince, I bear a message from your father."

My father! It felt like I hadn't heard from Rylan in quite a while, but that was probably just because of how busy we all had been. Everyone had more to do than time to do it in. I looked at my friends, unsure of what to do, and said, "Very well. Thank you for coming all this way. What message does he send me?"

The other messenger looked up at me, and I saw concern in her eyes. She said, "King Rylan instructed us to tell you that he needs you back in Ochana, urgently. Dragons are vanishing all over the world, and he needs you at his side if we're to keep the order and peace in Ochana."

The man added, "They're scared, my prince. We are to bring you home immediately, and hope it is in time."

Chapter Seventeen

It took a couple days, but we were finally close enough to see beautiful Ochana, home and safe at last. Its enchanted waterfall, flowing forever into the clouds below, still mesmerized me every time I saw it. My thoughts drifted to when I'd first learned to fly, spending hours zipping in and out of those falling waters or just letting them carry me down into the clouds. I'd fall through and just drift down, until I got bored and spread my wings, ready to fly back up and ride the waters down again. Nice times that felt like they were in another lifetime.

I shook my head, clearing my thoughts, and glanced behind me. Dragon eyes could see a long, long way, like an eagle's. The Woland Realm was flying as fast as they could but were still a couple miles behind us. It was hard for them to keep up since they had to carry the tied-up, freaked-out, psycho murder-dragon. That guy still hadn't calmed down. I was surprised he hadn't summoned his human because if he had, he could have escaped the ropes easily. I guessed he hadn't thought of it.

Jericho's voice rang in my head: "Pay attention to where you're going, Cole. You almost ran into Cairo. Don't worry about the dragon back there. Our people will figure out what's wrong with him, I'm sure. We're almost home."

I looked ahead again. We were getting close enough that we had to slow down, which was why I'd almost hit Cairo when I wasn't paying attention. We turned and decelerated, circling as we came down toward the landing area. People were gathered there, waiting, and Rylan and Sila were with them. They stood to one side, waiting for me to land. I was actually excited to see them again.

Jericho insisted we keep circling to let the Second Realm land first with the crazy dragon. Only after the Realm touched down and were human again did we finish our own descent. I summoned my human just as my feet hit the stone pavement, shifting smoothly.

Just as I'd imagined, my mother was right on top of me when I landed, wrapping me in her arms before I'd even come to a full stop. I put my arms around her, too, grinning. She kept it going just a little too long, so I started to feel kind of awkward.

Rylan said, "Enough, my love. Let our son go, you're embarrassing him." Then, when she grudgingly stepped back, he grinned at me and shook my hand. He was always the more proper of the two. I grinned back, thinking he would have tried to hug me if people weren't around.

Then Jericho was barking orders, getting the prisoner on the way to where they could safely study him. Maybe they had dragon-sized rubber rooms somewhere. I asked Rylan, "Where is he going? Something's really wrong with that guy."

Rylan nodded, watching Jericho and the others as they hauled the prisoner away. "Let's talk over lunch. I know you must be half-starved."

Sila added, "We have plenty of food set out in the great hall for you four, though Jericho will just have to take what's left. That man won't even sit down until everything is in order. He's quite diligent."

That was one way of putting it. I nodded but kept my smart-aleck comments to myself. I didn't want to wait even one more second to dig into the mountain of food that no doubt waited for us in the great hall. My stomach rumbled loudly, but my parents pretended not to notice. Eva, on the other hand, jammed her elbow into my ribs. "Well, let's get going before this one wastes away to nothing."

"Gee, thanks," I said as we followed the king and queen toward the castle.

An hour later, I sat in the great hall surrounded by a dozen empty serving trays that had once been mounded high with all sorts of meats, eggs, potatoes, and even a few veggies. I liked the carrots they grew in Ochana; they were the sweetest ones I'd ever tasted, but most dragons considered them to be just food for horses. I think Eva ate even more than me. Jericho was just getting started on his second platter of bacon and sliced ham as my meal settled.

My head was finally clearing from the hunger-fog, and I felt human again. Or dragon. Whatever. My mahier was coming back up to normal levels, too. Flying across Europe and half the Atlantic

Ocean without being seen took a lot of energy! I was grateful my parents let us eat before the questioning began.

"So," I said at last, patting my full stomach, "I'm sure you heard the reports we sent ahead, right?"

Rylan, sipping at a glass of wine but not eating much, nodded. "I'm frankly amazed. You've learned to use mereum and brought the Mere Treaty to life. You can cure the blackness, at least in a small area—which is a great start—and you uncovered the reason the Fairies attacked the Realm of dragons we'd sent to help guard their lands while you were gone."

"True," Eva said, "but then you summoned Cole home again all of a sudden. What is going on?"

Rylan sighed. "You'd think I'd be happier than I am."

That got my attention. I hadn't grown up with my father, but I knew enough to recognize an opening when he presented it. "Yeah, I would have thought so."

He replied, "Jericho has already heard this, but I wanted to tell you myself, not through a report. We have some very bad news to share with you, my son.

As Prince of Ochana, dealing with this will fall on your shoulders, too."

"Ooo-kay..." I raised an eyebrow at him. Why was he taking forever to get to the point? "Dealing with what, exactly?"

"We know why the Carnites and Dark Elves have been trying to capture you. It is not *you* they want, but all dragons. They have been catching as many as they can find, and then they're using dark magic to brainwash them. Eldrick is turning them into crazed monsters that only he can control through his mind powers, even halfway around the world."

My jaw dropped. All the times they'd tried to catch us, and failed... I could only imagine how many times they had succeeded if they were going after everyone outside of Ochana. "How many of the brainwashed ones have we saved?"

I wasn't sure why that was my first question, but I caught my mother's approving nod again.

"It is good that your first priority is our people's safety, son," Rylan said. "The truth is that we haven't been able to capture any, much less save them. We've been forced to kill a few, but most of them are attacking our allies, wreaking havoc, then flying away before anyone can rally the defenders. Your prisoner is the first anyone has captured. I think we may be able to catch more now, though, since you've found out how to do it."

Between big bites of meat, Jericho said, "We still haven't had any success breaking the connection between the prisoner and Eldrick. I do not know if we will ever be able to bring their minds back. Our people will keep working on the problem, of course."

Rylan nodded. "Of course. In the meantime, all of this has created another problem for us all, especially you, Son."

Sila said, "Any Prince of Ochana has duties to the people. The fact is, our people are in the middle of a full-blown panic. There's fear in every heart, as much as it pains me to see that. Our allies are in a panic, too, but our immediate problem is Ochana itself."

Rylan stood from his heavy chair and began pacing back and forth with his hands behind his back. His shiny boots clicked on the tile floor with every step. "Fear is what will tear us apart. As long as the people fear to stand up and do what's needed, we're going to have a hard time fighting this war, or even protecting ourselves."

"What can we do to help?" Eva asked. "We don't have any concrete plans, right now. We were supposed to 'find the source in the Fairy realm,' but I don't think we did that."

Rylan glanced at me and kept pacing. "Right now, the people of Ochana need their prince to lead them by his example."

"What can I do?" I asked.

"We need you to stay here and rally them." He turned to Eva and added, "He'll need your help, even if it's just to stand by his side so he has the strength to face them all."

Eva nodded. Of course, she would do that. I was relieved to hear she'd be staying with me.

Rylan stopped and turned to look me in the eyes and said, "You're not just the prince of Ochana. You are the Keeper of Dragons. If you go among them and tell them that everything will be well again, our people will listen to you."

I pursed my lips. I wasn't sure that was true. "And what do I tell them if it isn't well again soon? We don't know that we're going to win the war. Maybe we should at least be ready with a backup plan, just in case their prophecy is the one that turns out to be true. What will we do if we lose this war?"

Sila put her hands together on top of the table, lacing her long, slender fingers together. It made her look like a beautiful statue, the way she sat so straight and confident. She said calmly, "The people already know we could lose this. They feel it in their bones. Sometimes, as a leader, you must tell your people what they need to hear, not what they already know. It may be true we could lose, but it's also true we could win."

Rylan said, "That's what they are forgetting."

Sila continued, "Yes, and you must remind them of that fact, Son. Eldrick might have a prophecy about ruling the world, but Aprella gave us a different prophecy, the one where the Keeper of Dragons saves all True beings. I have faith that we will win."

Everyone stared at me, waiting for me to reply. I didn't really have much of a choice, though. My mother was right. I stood from my chair and put my hands on the table, leaning forward. "Ochana deserves that hope. As my father just said, we have a lot to be happy about, too. A lot to give us hope. Yes, of course, I'll stay and rally our people the best I can."

Rylan grinned, looking relieved, but Sila just smiled as though she knew there had never been any question what I'd do. I hoped I could live up to her faith in me.

Chapter Eighteen

I wanted to get a good feel for how my people were doing, but I couldn't do that just listening to my parents. Having a bunch of bodyguards following me could have kept me from getting people's honest thoughts, so I ditched them after lunch. I wanted the unfiltered truth.

Now I walked through the streets of Ochana, trying not to be too obvious as I eavesdropped on people talking. I blended in by wearing jeans and a gray hoodie—the hood kept people from catching on to who I was, but it also meant I had to get closer to overhear what people were talking about through the hoodie's fabric.

First, I went to the Great Library of Ochana. It always had lots of people sitting on the stone steps out front or laying around on the well-kept grass fields to either side. Most of them were my age or maybe a bit older, so it had a vibe like what I imagined a college campus would be like.

Since I couldn't eavesdrop on the people out in the grass—it would be too obvious—I focused on the stairs. I pretended like I was waiting for someone, leaning against the wall running up one side of the steps, halfway up. Just below me, two men and a woman sat together, leaning back and taking in the sunlight while they chatted. The first thing I noticed was that they weren't smiling. Shoulders hunched forward, looking down a lot, they seemed tense. The younger of the two men kept turning his head back and forth, scanning around him while they talked.

"We never should have gone back down there. The king made a mistake trying to help the Elves," the woman said.

The older guy said, "Are you kidding? If we'd been down there all along, like we should have been, this never would have happened. You want to blame a king? Blame the last one, not Rylan."

"Don't let anyone hear you talking about kings like that, you two," the younger man replied. "None of that matters, though. What happened can't be changed I'm just glad the prince is back. The Keeper will fix all this, you'll see. Aprella herself said so."

The woman, sitting between the men, nudged the younger one's arm with her elbow and said, "You mean if he is the Keeper at all. I mean, what are the odds the Keeper came right when we needed him? And what are the odds that our prince himself just so happened to be the Keeper? I think it's a PR stunt to keep us all from freaking out."

"No way, he's the Keeper. I heard he can use tilium *and* mereum. And there's a rumor he can kill off the black spots that Elf traitor created. Only the Keeper could do that, and the oracles have always said the Keeper will fix the Time of Fear."

The older man snorted, laughing and mocking the younger one. "You mean the king's pet oracle? Of course, she'll say what he tells her to, that's her job. They just don't want us freaking out, if you ask me."

The woman sat up and wrapped her arms around her knees. "Well, I'm plenty freaked out, so it didn't work. Ochana is next, you know. And stop talking about King Rylan like that. It's treason, and wrong. He's our leader, and way better than the last one."

I had heard enough. It was pretty much what I expected to hear, except for the part where one of them thought Rylan was faking the prophecy just to keep people calm. If one person said it, how many more people just thought it?

I wandered toward the market zone, hoping to hear more from an older crowd. Extra centuries of living might have given them a different perspective. I wandered down the steps and then crossed the main boulevard. Ten minutes later, I was in the market, surrounded by throngs of people. I was wrong about them all being old—there were plenty of younger dragons, too, and more than a few who must have been ancient.

But young, middle-aged, or old, the conversations I overheard were mostly the same. Everyone was terrified, and some were even scared enough to look at their king, feeling the need to place blame somewhere.

Just then, I bumped into a young man carrying packages, which he'd almost dropped when we walked into each other. "Oh sorry," I said and turned to move on.

"Prince," he said, startled. "I should be the one to apologize."

A woman nearby must have only heard part of our conversation because she turned and said, "Price Colton? Pah! He's trying, but he's too young to do this. Keeper of Dragons, indeed."

A merchant with a wagon stand handed the woman a paper-wrapped package and said, over the market noise, "He may be the Keeper, but the trouble came too soon. He doesn't have the experience to protect us. He can't help us now. You should stock up on food now, because who knows how long it'll be here."

More people spotted me. Some shook my hand, but most stayed back a little. They seemed unsure how to approach me. Was it because I was the prince, or because I was the Keeper? Maybe both. But as word spread, more people pressed toward me until I had a crowd around me. They called out questions. They begged me to protect their soldier sons. They asked more questions than I could answer.

But mostly, they simply doubted I could save them. I could *feel* how strong their fear was. It was stronger than their faith in their king, stronger than their common sense, even. So much fear from so many people... Their auras washed over me like a wave, and I started looking for a way out. Coming to the market had been a mistake. My father was right. Blending with them wasn't the way to lead them. I thought about calling everyone together to talk to them all at once from the king's audience platform, a grand stone ramp that stuck out from Ochana Castle so the king could address all his people. It would work just as well for a prince.

But then I stopped, mid-step, realizing that I wasn't really thinking about the best way to talk to them. No, I was just making excuses to justify running away from so many people who doubted me. I couldn't run away, not if I wanted those same people to follow me. Why follow a leader who talked *down* to them from some platform? I had to talk to them where they were, right where they lived. It was the only way to lead them, and leading them was the only way to banish all that fear that made them doubt their future. They needed hope more than they needed a speech.

I moved through the crowd, hearing people murmur as I went by them, and headed to an empty auctioneer's platform off to one side. It'd be high enough for people to see me, but close enough to actually talk to them, not talk down to them. I climbed the ladder and walked to the front of the platform.

From the crowd of market shoppers and merchants, someone shouted my name and pointed to the platform, and a murmur went up as a hundred heads turned, every eye on me as they wondered what I'd do and why I was there. The cry carried beyond the crowd, too, and more and more people began coming to see what was going on. Two hundred people were staring at me, but in minutes it became three hundred. I wanted to shrink under so many eyeballs! I was terrified, really, but I couldn't show it. They didn't need to see me scared like everyone else—they needed a leader. That's why my father had brought me back to Ochana, after all. I'd just have to do it my way, not how he'd wanted me to. I wasn't a leader, but I could fake it for them.

Plus, if I messed up, it wasn't like the whole island would see it the way they would if I choked on a speech from up in the castle's platform. Up there, a thousand cameras would be on me and every dragon in Ochana would see it. The more I realized that it could be a practice speech, the more confident I felt. I squared my shoulders, looked out over the sea of faces, and smiled. Giving a speech was also kind of exciting, even if it was terrifying.

Someone shouted, "Silence, the prince wants to speak," but the noise didn't die down. If anything, it got louder as people started arguing about what I'd say.

I took a deep breath and stepped up to the railing, ready to shout out to them, but I paused. I really wanted it to seem like I was talking to each one of them, not just to a crowd. An idea hit me. Mereum was everywhere—Ochana lived up in the clouds, and the mist from its never-ending waterfall was a light fog. I had all the mereum I could ever need.

I focused my will on the mereum, not gathering it up like normal but channeling it, using it to carry my words to each person in the crowd. With that, I could talk normally. Plain old Cole having a pleasant chat. Yet, they'd all hear me like I stood next to them. Kind of impressed with my idea, I grinned, and saw the people up front grinning back at me. That helped take my stage fright away, too.

"Yes," I began, and adjusted how the mereum carried the sound so it would be a little louder, "I'm Prince Cole. Whatever rumors you've heard otherwise, I am the Keeper of Dragons. You hear me now like I'm standing beside you because I'm controlling mereum in the air to bring my words to you without having to shout. I want to talk to you, just one dragon from Ochana to another."

I had things I needed to tell them, but with my stage fright barely under control, I wasn't really sure what I was saying. The words just spilled out, almost like I was on auto-pilot. After that, I just sort of let my mouth do its thing.

I told them about the things I'd seen. I talked about fighting at the side of an Elven prince and a

Fairy queen, a Troll king and a dragon chimera. I told them about the evil I'd seen Eldrick do, the people he'd killed.

But I also told them about how we rescued the Trolls from him. I almost shouted when I told them about the fight with the Farro, and how it felt to take their tilium from them and then defeat them. Permanently!

I pulled out the Mere Blade itself, letting it shine brightly over my head so they could see the awesome magical sword glowing.

I told them about fighting Carnites hand-to-hand, and how it felt to crush them. I talked about my personal fight with Eldrick, who tried to kill me with his visions, and how I not only survived but used the connection *he* created to help defeat his plots one after another.

I told them how it felt to bridge the rifts we dragons had created, bringing back our old alliances with other races of Truth. Together, they were all stronger than any crazy Dark Elf madman, and coming together, mighty Ochana could face any challenge. It was the *only* way we could ever win; it was the best way we'd always won before.

By the time I finished, the crowd was cheering my name. It had gone from being a speech to feeling like a school rally as they pulled together!

That was when I realized there were way more people around me than when I had started. The sun was lower than it had been. I must have been talking to them for an hour or more.

But the biggest shock came when I turned around to climb down the ladder. Suddenly, I saw myself displayed on the inside of the magic dome protecting Ochana as if it were a huge screen. I stared at it, frozen. I had totally forgotten the city had technology that was years ahead of anything I'd seen growing up among humans. I'd been televised on that jump screen to everyone, all over the island. My practice speech had been the real deal!

And judging by how the crowd here was cheering me, it must have worked. I'd spoken from the heart, and they responded. The jumbo-screen faded away, but the cheering didn't. I slid down the ladder to the waiting crowd. I shook hands and answered questions until long past dusk, well into the night. Ochana's whole aura had changed, and mine with it.

It was a long evening, but despite how late it was when I got to bed, I still had a hard time sleeping. I was just too excited, too wired up. Somehow, I'd made a difference to Ochana's people with one heartfelt speech. It was a lesson I swore I'd always remember.

Chapter Nineteen

Shortly after breakfast, three days after my weird and amazing speech, Jericho summoned me to a council meeting. The messenger let me know the king and queen, Eva, and Cairo had also been summoned, but he didn't know what the meeting would be about.

I thanked him, then looked through my dresser for more appropriate clothes. I'd been wearing jeans and hoodies for the last few days, which I'd been spending out among the people, talking to them where they lived and worked instead of on a jumbo monitor. Obviously, Jericho had something important to say, and I could practically hear his commander voice barking orders at me about how "playtime was over."

I let out a long sigh as I put on a set of clothes that looked remarkably like a uniform, yet wasn't. Rylan once told me that looking like a leader was half of actually being one, and I didn't really look forward to Jericho ordering me around like usual. Maybe if I looked like I outranked him, he wouldn't be as bossy. Come to think of it, I really did outrank him. That had never seemed to help me much before, though.

I was the last to arrive. The only elder present other than my father was Jericho. I'd expected the other councilors to be there, which could only mean that this would be a military meeting. A war council. But then, why were Eva and Cairo there? I'd find out soon enough.

I stepped into the room, waved at Eva, nodded to Cairo, then sat next to my father and faced Jericho across the table.

The wily general smiled and said, "Thank you for coming. I'll get right to the point and tell you why I called this war meeting." So, it was to be a war meeting, after all.

"You're welcome," I said, enjoying his irritated glance. He hadn't expected a response.

Instead of sparring with me, though, he got right back to what he wanted to talk about. "Eldrick seems to be gathering his troops. Reports show them moving all around the world, heading this way. Since most of his troops are on foot, it will take them at least a month or two to gather, but I think he's getting ready to make his move."

Rylan frowned. "What are we doing about this?"

"I've had my staff working around the clock preparing for our final stand. They'll keep doing that until time runs out, however long that may be." He paused to let that sink in, looking each of us in the eyes one at a time. "It is my belief that we should ask the other races to form an accord with us, *before* Eldrick attacks—"

"Wait." Rylan interrupted him.

My father was larger-than-life, always standing straight and proud like a king, or like a conquering general. He was used to being in charge, and history had shown he was right far more often than not. He was also the kind of person others naturally followed, even in battle. A born leader. So when he interrupted, he hadn't even had to raise his voice to silence the room. We all turned to look at him.

He continued, "I think your plan is too risky, old friend. The peace we've created with them is still fragile. It hasn't been long enough to start asking for their help, not like this. They have fresh memories of us refusing to come to their aid when my father ruled Ochana, and they have their own battles to fight."

Jericho bowed his head in respect. "Yes, my king. But times are different from when your father was king."

"Yes, they are. The peace is delicate now, and it wasn't then. Not until we turned our backs on them. If we'd come to their aid then, Eldrick would never have survived his attempt to take over the Elves. And every other race knows that."

Jericho's eyes burned red. "Yes, the new peace is fragile. I know asking for help might send *some* of them running to look after themselves. But the rest will honor the accord."

Rylan growled. "How is sending some of our allies running away what you want us to do? Give the alliance time to set! Then ask for help."

"Because some won't run! I'm telling you as plainly as I can, my king, that if Eldrick attacked us right now, he'd win. He'd push through our defenses in hours, and it would all be over for us. That is what we've been analyzing these last couple days."

Rylan shook his head and put both hands flat on the table, his thumbs touching, and looked into Jericho's stony eyes without flinching. "Eldrick may not attack today or even this year. If you pull in our half-hearted allies, some will stop being our allies. And what of the rest? Should they just sit in Ochana until Eldrick gets around to attacking us?"

No one would interrupt the king, of course, but I really wanted to cut in with a dozen questions. Yet the more I thought about those questions, the more I realized I already knew the answers. It was weird, when I'd first learned I was a dragon, I would have asked anyway. I wouldn't have had any confidence in my own answers. I had come a long way in the last few months, it seemed.

"Cole!" Rylan snapped.

I spun to face him, feeling my face grow warm. "Yes, Father?"

"I asked you a question. Well?"

I wanted to run and hide. I hadn't even heard his question! I was too deep in my own thoughts when he asked. "Um, what was the question?"

Rylan rolled his eyes, but my mother put her hand on his, stopping him from snapping back. She said, "You're the prince of Ochana, someday our king, and you're the Keeper of Dragons. What do you think? The two best military minds in Ochana disagree on what to do, and maybe the Keeper can help us find the way. He asked for your decision."

"My decision?" I wanted to shrink away and hide. I'd just been thinking about how much more confident and capable I'd grown. It was ironic.

Rylan let out a deep breath. "She's right. You must make the final decision. You are the one who keeps the balance. Do we shatter our new alliances without a second thought, or do we do the smart thing and wait for them to get stronger before we ask for their help?"

I recognized that stubborn tone. It was the same one I'd used a hundred times before. It was kind of interesting in how many ways he and I were so similar even though I'd grown up among the humans, not on Ochana with him.

I already knew my answer, though.

"If the final decision is up to me, then I say it's best that we ask for help now, while we still can. Eldrick won't wait as long as you hope, Father. Anything else is wishful thinking. He knows how weak we are because he's the one who made us that way. He's coming as soon as he thinks he has enough troops, not waiting for every last Carnite to get to Alaska."

Jericho nodded, and he looked at me like he was seeing me for the first time. Before Rylan could snap back at me, Jericho said, "Very well, Prince. Eva and Cairo will go to the Fairies and ask their help. Clara and I will go to the Elves and Trolls and see if we can get Gaber and Evander to see reason."

Sila said, "We should send Luka, Jules, and Allas to the Mermaids. They'll respect us more with them going to ask."

Jericho smiled and inclined his head to her. "Yes, excellent thinking. Cole will stay here and continue to rally the people. After that speech he made," he said, grinning at me, "he'll be of best use here."

Rylan slowly rose, but he didn't look as angry as I'd feared. "I don't think this is a wise plan, Cole. But very well, so be it. Each group will also take a battalion of dragons to escort those who ally themselves with Ochana. They'll need help getting here. Aprella only knows how you expect Eldrick to get an army here when our own allies need help to get here themselves."

I shook my head at him. I wasn't going to let him talk us out of this. "It may be risky, but it's safer than sitting here hoping Eldrick doesn't find some way to get into Ochana. He did it before, and if he's gathering his troops, it's because he has a plan to do it again. This is the only chance we've got."

I sounded more confident than I felt, just like with my speech to the people. The truth was, I wasn't sure we had a chance at all. I couldn't just sit back and wait for the end, though. It was better to go down fighting.

Chapter Twenty

I stood on my balcony high above Ochana, looking out over my beautiful city. I wasn't sure when I had started to think of it as my city, or when Paraiso had started seeming like a vacation. Glorious, beautiful, natural, but just a vacation. Those are never meant to last forever. As much as I wanted to help Paraiso, Ochana now felt like where I *belonged*. Getting exiled had been the swift kick in the pants I needed to realize it, that's all.

The sound of my sliding glass door opening dragged me from my thoughts. I recognized Rylan's presence behind me. "Father. It's beautiful, isn't it? Ochana, I mean."

"As it has been for more centuries than I can count," he said, almost whispering. "I stand on my balcony, too, when things are bothering me. It helps me put it into perspective. So what is troubling you today?" He stepped up beside me on the balcony and leaned against the railing, looking out as well.

"It's just easier to be alone when I'm up here like this," I said. I wasn't sure that was exactly right, but it was close enough to how I was feeling.

"Your friends have been gone a few days, but you're hardly alone."

I shook my head. Rylan was wrong about that. I felt alone in a crowded room, sometimes. "I've kept busy doing all I can, preparing our people for war if it comes to that, but when I stop for the night, I do feel alone. These are my people, but they don't truly know me. Like I don't really know them. It has only been a few months since I thought dragons and Elves were myths and humans were the top of the food chain."

Rylan was quiet for a long moment, and we just stood together on my balcony and looked down on the beautiful city. At last, though, he said, "A king is always lonely. Every one of these people is our responsibility. Even our friends. There will always be that part of you that knows your friends are also your burden and responsibility. But that doesn't make them any less your friends, Son. It makes them the motivation I use to keep going, to keep fighting and putting my people ahead of myself. Maybe they are for you, too."

"Wow. That's deep. I wonder if that's why your father turned his back on the world. Maybe he just couldn't bear the thought of something bad happening to any of his people."

Rylan's hands gripped the railing a little tighter. "I had never really thought of it like that. I guess our friends do more than give us a reason to put others ahead of ourselves. Maybe they also give us the perspective we need so that we don't make the mistakes my parents made when they ruled this kingdom. They... didn't have a lot of friends outside the family."

Maybe he was right. I didn't know what to say, so I just nodded.

"Cole, I want you to know that I'm proud of you. The role you've taken isn't what I had in mind for you, but it suits you. In the time you were away from here, traveling, you somehow found the strength and courage to become a leader. Your friends and your people, they all follow you now. It's not because they have to, and not because you were born in charge, but because of who you are. I think you may become a better leader than I have been, if you aren't already. Don't tell your mother I said that."

I snorted, but then I paused. Was he wrong? It didn't feel like I had been a good leader. So many people had died, and I couldn't save them. Sure, we saved some of the Trolls, but not enough to save their kingdom or the Earth. Dragons were supposed to lead all the races of Truth, but so far, my track record with that hadn't been great.

I found myself fidgeting with the ring that the spirit Prince Jago gave me. I wished he hadn't chosen me. I didn't think I deserved it, and there was a shadow in my mind that kept telling me I wasn't good enough, I wasn't going to save them, and I wasn't going to save the world. I was pretty sure I was going to fail at that, just like I'd failed to save the Trolls.

And I had to try anyway.

I didn't tell my dad any of that, though. We talked about nicer things for a while, maybe the first small talk I'd had with him, but eventually he had to go. He was the king, and he had duties he couldn't ignore.

When he was gone, I felt just as lonely as I did before he showed up. My responsibilities were heavy on my mind. One of those responsibilities was to our wounded. There weren't many, not yet, but the dragon we captured was one of them. Almost without thinking about it, I found myself heading directly to Ochana's hospital wing. I just needed to see if there had been any change in his condition. He was a monster now, but he'd been a good dragon before that.

When I got there, I went up to the front counter. The administrator had been looking at her monitor, but when she saw who I was, she blushed. "I'm so sorry, Prince Colton. I didn't realize it was you, and I have more work to do than time. I should have paid better attention. What can we do for you?"

I put a smile on my face, mostly for her benefit. "I didn't mean to interrupt. I wanted to come see the dragon I brought with me from the Fairy realm. Has he gotten any better?"

When she flinched and set down the notepad she'd been holding, I thought the answer was going to be bad. When she stepped out from behind the counter and put her hand on my arm, I knew it was.

"I'm sorry. We haven't figured out yet how to cure him. We have people working on it twenty-four hours a day, though. The king made sure of that. But we're starting to think that there is no way to save him. If the magic is strong enough, only Eldrick's death can save this dragon, or the dozens like him who are still out there suffering."

"Can I see him?" I didn't know why I felt like I needed to, but I did.

"Yes, of course. You can't go into his cell, but we have a one-way glass set in the wall. You can see him, but he won't see you. It's for our safety."

"Of course. Thank you." I followed her to the cell and then could only stare at the monster inside. His body was a dragon's, but his mind felt like a wounded animal's to my mahier senses. Part of me hoped his mind really wasn't in there somewhere, watching himself like an outsider, even if that meant there was hope to save him. I wasn't sure which would be a worse fate.

I stayed there with him for hours, watching him, wishing that my being there was enough to help, somehow. I knew it wasn't, though.

When the facility's visiting hours ended that night, I headed back to the castle. I locked myself in my room and for once, I was glad my friends were gone. I needed to be alone after seeing the prisoner. I needed time to come to grips with it.

Hours later, I drifted off to sleep.

I dreamed of explosions. When I awoke, sweating, I sat bolt upright in bed and put my hands over my ears as I focused on slowing my heartbeat. I waited for the sleep fog to fade away so I could get back to sleep—

Then I heard more explosions. It was no dream, I realized with a sinking feeling in my chest. I ran to my balcony and looked out. That view had once given me a bit of comfort looking out over the beauty of Ochana. Now, it was full of smoke and fire, not comfort. All over the city, dragons swarmed, carrying Dark Elves and even Carnites on their backs. They landed and dropped off their cargoes, then rose into the air again. Fires raged and lightning forked the sky, and dragons flew through the air, thick as a swarm of bees.

Eldrick was attacking with so many forces, I couldn't begin to count them. So many dragons carrying so many soldiers... We didn't have months, after all. I felt my stomach flip-flopping. Ochana was doomed.

Chapter Twenty-One

I slapped myself a couple of times to wake myself up. With the sounds of battle coming through the window, I ran across the room to my gear. Most of it was in a wall locker, except my armor, which was displayed on a mannequin. I hated taking the time to put the armor on, but it was no time to be running around unprotected.

The breastplate looked like scales, and I'd been told they were actual dragon scales tied to hardened leather—immune to fire, almost impossible to cut. Smaller bits, also scaled, went over my shoulders and covered my upper arms. My shins were covered by engraved black metal plates, called greaves. There was also a skirt-looking thing made of a lot of long leather strips, covered in scales like the breastplate. The scaled, leather strips hung down from a belt I could wear over my clothes, protecting everything down to my knees without limiting my movement at all.

I threw on a pair of boots, grabbed the Mere Blade, and at the last minute, put on my helmet. It was made of engraved black metal, like the shin greaves. It covered not only my head but also the back of my neck. It had metal flaps hanging down to cover my cheeks, and a thin strip of metal hung down between my eyes to protect my nose. It was just as uncomfortable as it sounded.

When I opened my door, I came face-to-face with two Wolands. They wore full plate mail armor, heavier than mine, and their helmets covered their entire heads and faces, like medieval knights.

"My prince," one said, "the entire west end of Ochana is under attack. We have to get you to the safe room. Jericho gave us orders to protect you at all costs. King Rylan and Queen Sila are there already."

I stared at them in disbelief for a second. They wanted the prince to hide while the kingdom burned. Um, no? I'd been through too much to run away and hide now. "I can't run and—"

"Sir, we have to go *now* if we have any hope of getting you there at all. The attackers are pushing through our defenses already!"

My mind raced. From the safe room, all I could do was wait until Eldrick killed every defender and then he'd blast the royal family out or blow us up. The protection of the safe room would slow him down, but it wouldn't stop him from getting to us forever.

The thought struck me once again that I outranked Jericho. Maybe not when it came to defending Ochana, but I could bully my way through the guards... maybe. Plus, at the moment, Jericho wasn't in Ochana to give them other orders. Well, it was time to take my authority as prince out for a spin.

"No. I order you to come with me. Go to the safe room if you're too afraid to fight, but I won't run while our people are out there dying. I don't know about you, but I'm tired of running anyway."

I pushed my way past them and then ran down the hall, whether they followed me or not.

Thankfully, they didn't try to stop me by force and instead ran with me.

As we came around a corner up ahead, there were other people rushing toward us, wearing hooded cloaks. They were dragons, but were they friendly or were they more of the crazed ones? I pulled my sword, and my guards did the same as they stepped in front of me.

The lead oncoming dragon stopped ten feet away and pulled back the hood covering his face. It was my Uncle Zane! I let out a whoop of joy.

"Cole," he said, saluting me, "I came right away. We can't let Eldrick capture you. The Keepers have to get out alive for the prophecy to come true. We have to get you out of here."

I shook my head as I slid my sword back into its scabbard. "No. If you want to make sure I stay alive, then you'll just have to come with me and do what you can to protect me. Bring your guards."

"What? Why? By Aprella, we have to get to the safe room." Zane's left eyelid twitched.

"No, we have to alert the east end of the island and rally our people out there. They may not yet even know we're under attack and they'll be sitting ducks."

"But Cole—"

"I'm going. You can stay here or come with me, whatever. It's been good seeing you, Zane, but my people are waiting for me." I took off running down the hall.

My two guards called after me, but I didn't slow down. I heard many boots behind me, clomping on the stone floor, and I smiled when I realized Zane was coming with me, along with our eight soldiers—my two in plate mail and his six armored in breastplates like Zane and me, but with chainmail everywhere else. I hoped eight soldiers would be enough to do what I had in mind, even with Eldrick's troops pouring in fast.

The ten of us ran east, dodging the enemy troops, who seemed to be scattered across the west end of Ochana. I used my mahier to keep anyone from seeing us, but that meant the good guys didn't see us, either. Only once we were well away from the fighting did I let the mask fall, and then we got busy raising the alarm and rousing everyone.

I wondered why Ochana's main alarms weren't going off, and suspected sabotage.

We went house to house after splitting up to cover ground faster. Every time I found someone home, after they got whatever battle gear they owned ready, I had them run off to find yet more people. And so on. The crowd quickly grew.

In less than half an hour, we had most of Ochana roused and dressed for war. Once that was almost done, I had to start gathering the troops, though. I took a deep breath and then focused my mind on sending a message to all my nearby people. "Join me at Rylan Square. To arms!" I concentrated on sending that message out, over and over. I wasn't sure whether my telepathy would be strong enough, but when mobs of armed dragons began coming to the square, I knew it had.

Rylan Square was a beautiful place, like a park, and I was told they changed the name every time a new king was crowned. If we survived the day, the park would someday be called Colton Square, but first, we had a job to do.

In the distance, the sounds of battle got more intense as Eldrick ferried fresh troops down. I didn't know how he had gotten through our defenses, but I suspected Zane had something to do with that. Hopefully, it was from back when Zane once pretended to join the enemy. We'd done a lot of damage to Eldrick's allies because of it, eliminating the Farro and taking their tilium, but Eldrick had learned more than Zane intended. He'd clearly saved some of that information until he was ready to attack Ochana with everything he had.

The alternative was that Zane really was a traitor, and had only pretended to be on our side again. If that was the case, I figured we were all doomed, so I really hoped he wasn't a traitor still. I hoped, but I wasn't going to turn my back to him just yet either.

My thoughts were interrupted when a dragon came swooping in from the west and a hundred of my dragons drew weapons at the same time. When he landed, though, he summoned his human form and saluted. So, he wasn't one of Eldrick's crazy, brainwashed dragons.

Zane said, "What news, soldier?"

The soldier's eyes were wide with fear, and he had a cut on his left cheek. He looked dirty and tired from fighting. He saluted and said, "Prince Colton, I spotted a company of Carnites coming this way. They went around us, going to the island's north end to get past our defenders, and I saw you in the distance so I came to warn you. Thank Aprella you got these people together already, or it would have been a slaughter."

I put my hand on his shoulder firmly, nodding. "Good job. So, we have a dozen Carnites headed our way? Um...Take a dozen of these dragons and go cut the Carnites off."

"Prince, these aren't trained soldiers. What can they do?"

"They'll fight. Listen, there are sleepers, children, and those too old to fight still hiding in these houses. I won't leave until they're safe, so I need time. You have to buy me time. Figure out how to make it work."

He grit his teeth, saluted me, then began collecting whatever dragons looked strong enough, whatever their color. Every dragon was a warrior today.

I turned to Zane and said, "Start getting the rest of these people into squads and send them west."

"Any instructions for them?"

I thought for a second, then said, "By the time they get close enough to join the battle, someone in HQ should see them and give them orders telepathically, right?"

"HQ has their hands full, or they'd have done the job we're doing."

He might have been right, so I said, "If they don't get orders when they get to the battle, make sure each unit has someone in charge to decide where they should go fight. Things look really chaotic out there, so they might need to come up with ideas on the fly. But if nothing else, they can fight their way toward Ochana Castle or the HQ."

Zane grunted and then started barking orders to the dragons we'd gathered. They looked terrified, especially the ones who weren't Wolands, but when he started telling them what to do, they listened. What else could they do? Hide? The war would come to them one way or another, so hiding wasn't an option. We had to keep Eldrick in the west end if we wanted to keep the kids and elder dragons as safe as possible. Most of the dragons actually looked relieved to have someone telling them what they should be doing.

Another messenger showed up, a woman in battered armor. She told me about a new enemy break-though. I grabbed four of the latest squads Zane had organized and sent them off with the messenger.

Then another dragon showed up, needing more squads. And another messenger, and another. We kept sending out units as fast as we could organize them, rushing to keep up with the demand. Ochana was being overrun. We needed to figure out a better plan, but I was kept busy dealing with enemy units breaking through our lines faster than I could get new units organized. It was frustrating. We started to get sloppy with our orders because things were happening too fast to think it through before just throwing units at them.

A real battle, I realized, was uncontrolled chaos. I was quickly learning what leaders did in battle, and it wasn't running off to fight. That would have been a relief, but as much as I wanted to go fight, I was doing more good for Ochana where I was.

All around us, more and more small battles were breaking out. A dozen dragons fought Dark Elves here, fifty fought Carnites over there. Angry roars, shouted orders, and the clanging sounds of swords hitting shields echoed through the city.

Then, I heard a high-pitched cry of pain behind me in the distance, carrying over the noise of battle. I turned to look. A few blocks away, I was horrified to see a big group of stooped, old dragons, along with kids in what looked like white paper robes. For a moment, it felt like time slowed to a crawl. I zoomed in with my mahier and dragon eyes, and realized the robes really were paper because they were actually hospital gowns. A Carnite had two of the kids, one in either hand, but when it threw one down like it was spiking a football, the kid's high-pitched scream stopped suddenly. I felt like throwing up. My people were getting mowed down, even the helpless elderly dragons and sick children.

I didn't hesitate—I was already sprinting toward the massacre, running past Zane as he turned to see where I was going. I heard him roar, outraged, but my only thought was to help the terrified, helpless dragons and punish the foul things that were hurting them.

Chapter Twenty-Two

I hit the nearest Carnite like a freight train and cut him down. The magical Mere Blade went through him like a hot knife through butter, and he toppled to the ground, dead before he hit.

The other Carnites, seeing their buddy go down, turned to me and roared. It was terrifying to look up at those giants and their spiked tusks, all of them staring at me with hatred. Their faces shifted from anger to fear, which confused me for a moment, but then I heard dragon roars and heavy footsteps behind me. A wave of armed dragons—red, blue, green, and even silver—surged past me, flowing around me as they charged the Carnites.

The Carnites were big and mean, but they were cowards. Before the armed dragon mob reached them like a swarm of ants attacking a beetle, the Carnites fled. The helpless dragons who had been the Carnites' victims cheered wildly.

I didn't feel like cheering, though, because when the Carnites fled, it revealed half a dozen dragons who were killed before I could save them. It could have been so much worse, I knew, but it still felt horrible.

The survivors all turned to look at me, desperate for someone to give them orders. I could see the panic written on their faces. My mind raced, but I didn't know what to say or do. The only thing I knew for sure was that I had to get them moving away from here. Doing *something* was better than standing around trying to figure out the *best* thing. Waiting around would only get more people killed.

So, I went with the first idea that hit me. "Zane, we've already cleared a path in the north end, right? Let's bring this mob that way. If we can get these kids, sick, and elderly dragons into the caves behind the waterfall, they can hide and wait out the battle." I pointed toward the beautiful mountain that had been the very first thing I'd seen in Ochana my first time here. It had a special place in my heart because of that, and it was kind of ironic that the same mountain might now save a lot of lives. But only if we could get them to it safely.

Zane said, "We'll have to fight our way through, but we'll have to fight if we stay here, too. Are you sure that's the best place to take them?" He looked tense, ready to burst into action as soon as I gave him the go-ahead.

I looked up, but all over the sky were far too many crazed, mind-controlled dragons to have my people risk trying to fly out. Most of the older ones didn't look strong enough to carry the kids on their best day, much less on a crazy, desperate ride for their lives.

"No, I'm not sure. But I *am* sure that if we stay here, we're done. Get them moving." I didn't wait for him to reply. I grabbed a couple squads of our assembled dragons, too young or too old to be soldiers but not to fight for their lives, and ran north with them. I had to trust Zane to get the rest of the mob moving, which I didn't like, but someone had to make sure the path was clear. I had told him it was, but I couldn't be sure it had stayed that way since the first messenger had come through there looking for reinforcements.

We ran through block after block of little dragon houses, corner parks with empty playgrounds, and small shops no one had opened today. They were all empty, and everything was creepy-silent except for faint battle noises from the west.

When we got closer to Ochana's north edge, we turned left, hoping to go around the worst of the fighting. The rest of the mob was only a hundred yards behind me, which was good. Zane had organized them quickly, so they wouldn't get too far behind.

A shadow fell over me and I ducked. It was pure reflex, but it saved my life as a huge, spiked club whooshed by me where my head had been. Carnites! Two dragons behind me had already jumped onto the one who attacked me, and they put the Carnite down. Two other Carnites were also quickly killed, though we lost one dragon who was too old and slow to dodge the Carnite's huge war club.

"Keep them moving!" I shouted without wasting any time. When Zane gave me a thumbs-up sign in reply, I ran ahead again with the ones I'd gathered, who included the guards who had started out with us—the few real soldiers we had. We made our way through the north neighborhood thick with small old houses and narrow, winding alleys. It gave us lots of cover, and before long, we came to the mountain.

My dragons started assisting the helpless people Zane and I waved through, rushing them to move faster into the caves behind the waterfall. It took a few scary, tense minutes to get everyone inside, and I felt like I didn't breathe again until they were out of sight inside.

From the entrance, Zane shouted, "Stay out of the council chambers. It doesn't have a roof, remember. The enemy will see you in there."

I recalled one tunnel I'd walked with Rylan which had spears and swords in racks lining both walls. I told Zane, "Gather up whoever is healthy enough to swing a sword or carry a spear, and get weapons from the displays by the council chambers. If Dark Elves get into the tunnels, you'll be the last line of defense and you'll need every armed dragon you can get."

He saluted sharply. "You can count on me. I wish we'd met under better circumstances, Cole. Your parents talked about you, always—I want you to know that."

I understood. This was our goodbye moment. The odds seemed pretty good that one or even both of us might not live through the day. I saluted back, then stuck out my hand.

He shook his head and wrapped his arms around me in a bear hug. In my ear, he whispered, "Aprella be with you out there, Nephew."

When we pulled away, we looked each other in the eyes. I nodded. There was nothing left to say. He turned and started organizing the civilians, and I gathered what few real soldiers we had.

Near the cave entrance, I looked them over. Eight red dragon soldiers, armed and armored better than any soldiers in all of history, especially the two in plate mail. As bodyguards, their armor was enchanted with mahier like mine was. I knew we wouldn't all make it through the battle. They knew it, too, but I could see steely determination in their eyes and I felt proud to be a dragon like them at that moment.

"Listen up," I said, and paced back and forth in front of them.

They snapped to attention, heels together, arms straight down at their sides with their thumbs lined up with their pants seams, standing tall. "Yes, Sir!" they all said together.

"You already know it's total chaos out there, so we have to stick together above everything else. Fight side by side, covering the dragon next to you with your shield while they do the same for you."

"Just like we trained," one said.

"Yes, nothing is different. Now, if you checked with your mahier to sense the battle, you already know we need to get the Realms organized if we want a shot at winning. Eldrick hit us by surprise, so our defenses weren't set and now they're scattered all over the battlefield. We have to get them fighting together and falling back toward HQ H so we can get our front line back to being a line. Any questions?"

One stepped forward and said, " What do we do if we're attacked by those crazy dragons? Any one of them might be a friend, a brother, a sister. What then?"

I knew that question was going to come up because I'd been thinking about it, too. Even if they were mind-sick because of Eldrick, those were still my people. I'd been trying to think of something to do besides killing them, but judging by the way the other dragons were looking down at their feet, they all knew what my answer had to be.

With more confidence than I felt, I said, "We'll try to take them out of the fight without killing them. Focus on the Dark Elves and Carnites, instead. Remember, if Eldrick dies, we think his control dies, too. Killing him is going to be the only way to save them, or ourselves. Until then, you know how battle is. You don't always get to decide who you fight, and if it comes down to you or them..."

"Make it them."

"Yes," I said, "and when this is over, I swear to you, we'll give every single one of them the hero's funeral they deserve. Now, let's get out there, rally our brothers and sisters, and push these rats off Ochana, once and for all."

There was no cheering, but I hadn't expected any. There were quiet nods all around, and I gave them a few seconds to come to grips with the reality we all had to face if we hoped to win the battle.

Then I let out a long, deep breath, turned, and walked out of the caves. We snuck as far away from the waterfall as we could, as fast as we could. I felt dark tilium and mahier all around us as dragons overhead and Dark Elves all around us scanned the battlefield for enemies. It took a lot of my own mahier to keep us hidden, but I spent it happily to let my soldiers keep as much of their energy as they could. I had tilium and mereum to fall back on when my mahier ran out.

I had noticed that most of the fighting was in or around the huge plaza where dragons flying in usually landed. There were just too many enemies running around everywhere around us, though. Every dragon unit I sensed with my mahier was fighting two or three times as many dragons and Dark Elves. Ochana's troops were split up, which made it worse because it was like they each fought their own little battle. It wasn't two armies fighting each other, but one army fighting scattered mobs of defenders. We'd never win like that. Every time I saw a unit of dragons, I focused my thoughts at them, sending messages. Fall back. Gather together. Rally at the castle.

I led my little group of soldiers around the plaza's edge. We came out of an alleyway at the far end. I was startled half out of my skin when we practically tripped over a cluster of six dragons dressed in the blue uniforms of Realm Four. When I realized they were ours, I grinned and felt a flood of relief.

One of my soldiers called out, "Hail, Realm Four. Follow Prince Colton! We're pulling everyone back to get our defenses organized around the castle."

The Realm Four dragons, hearing him, turned and headed our way. Another six dragons wouldn't make much of a difference out there, in the grand scheme of things, but they'd bring my group up to fourteen. That would be enough to give me an advantage if we ran into a squad of Dark Elves or crazed dragons.

I grinned at the first one when they were about twenty feet away. "We sure are glad to see you guys."

The dragons didn't reply. They kept walking toward me. Something wasn't right... Their weapons! They didn't have any. Soldiers had weapons. I opened my mouth to shout an alarm, but never got the chance as the first one suddenly sprinted. I didn't even have time to bring my sword up before he crashed into me, shoulder-first, and it felt like I was hit by a truck. As I flew through the air, I heard the fight begin. I landed on my back and skidded a few feet before I came to a stop. The blow had knocked the wind out of me. I was thankful for my training, though, because I found myself already climbing to my feet, and I had somehow kept my grip on my sword.

I saw one of the dragons in blue kneeling on one of my dragon's backs, grabbing his hair in one fist. The dragon in blue had summoned enough of his dragon form to grow a big claw from the top of his other fist, like a dagger. He was about to stab that into the back of my soldier's head.

I roared and reached out with one hand, using mereum to hold his claw-fist back. He struggled against me with insane strength, and I immediately broke into a sweat from how much effort it took to hold him back. He was stronger than me, though; his wicked spike got closer and closer to my soldier's head. Desperately, I focused everything into stopping him, but my control was slipping fast and the dragon hadn't weakened at all, yet.

A sword seemed to grow out of the crazed dragon's chest, covered in his blood. The skewered dragon had a split second where I saw the light come back into his eyes, and he looked down at the sword sticking out of his chest with a confused look. A moment later, he toppled to one side and fell to the ground. He didn't move again.

Breathing heavily, I looked up at my soldier who'd killed him. He put his foot on the fallen dragon's back and pulled hard on his sword, muscles flexing, trying to get his stuck blade free. A moment later, it came loose suddenly and he staggered back a step.

As I climbed to my feet again, I saw that only six of my eight dragons were still standing. The other two soldiers and the four crazed dragons in blue lay on the cobblestone road. My mahier senses told me that none of the fallen ones had heartbeats. I wanted to scream. Or cry. Maybe both. I'd just lost two loyal, good dragons at the very moment I had thought we were getting reinforcements. There was safety in numbers, but now I had fewer dragons with me, not more.

I glared at the closest soldier and snarled, "Why were those dragons dressed like our soldiers? Answer me!"

I knew he didn't deserve to be yelled at, and that he probably felt just the same way I did, but I couldn't help myself. I felt my eyes well up and tears fell, crawling down my cheeks. I'd never wanted to kill Eldrick more than I did at that moment, with fire in my veins.

The soldier looked at me, first with irritation written on his face, but then his expression melted into a sympathetic look as he spotted my tears. Instead of snapping back or saying anything to embarrass me, he turned to the other soldiers and shouted, "Grab their dog tags. All of them, even the ones we killed. We'll make sure those tags get back to HQ with us, understand? That's our mission. Now, move it, our prince can't wait all day for you lazy dragons!"

The others quickly knelt down by whichever body was closest. In a few seconds, they had all the tags, and they handed them to the one who had barked orders.

He then turned to me with the fistful of dog tags, gripping their thin chains so the tags dangled down and tinkled as they bumped one another. He held them out to me and said, "Sir, as you ordered, here are their IDs. Now we can give them a proper burning ceremony even if the enemy takes their bodies, or if we have to retreat from Ochana without them."

He gave me a faint smile as I took the tags in one hand and wiped my cheeks dry with my other hand. "Thank you," I said, feeling kind of ashamed for snapping at him. My thanks was for more than the dog tags, but also for his understanding, and because I felt a weird kind of relief to be around people whom I had fought beside when our dragons died. It was as if so long as we remembered them together, they weren't actually dead. Not truly.

For the next hour, we made our way through Ochana, hiding and running. We did find more soldiers to join us, and we lost more, but by the time I'd gotten the plaza cleared and our scattered army to fall back to get reorganized, I had two squads with me.

Unfortunately, the enemy had also reorganized and they were pushing hard at us. Ochana's defenders were doing better than before because I'd given HQ actual units to send orders to instead of scattered individual units. It helped us to react better and faster to new threats, but we were still far too outnumbered. They were pushing us back as fast as we could back up, and I knew it was only a matter of time.

Most of Ochana's army had been pressed back until they were in a thick line around HQ, but some units were cut off by the enemy line—including mine.

My squads and I finished off the last of an enemy squad of dark Elves—thankfully not our mind-controlled brothers and sisters—when I looked up in time to see more coming around a corner at the end of the block. I turned to lead my soldiers the other way, but more Dark Elves were already coming around that corner, too. We were trapped between them. The only way out would be a mad dash off the street and through empty houses and their tiny yards.

I flung my mahier senses out all around us to find the safest path, but all I saw were more Dark Elves in every direction. There wasn't a way out.

"All right, dragons, listen up! We'll run south from here, through that blue house across the street. I'll kick in the door, and don't wait for me before you start running through it. Go out the back, then hightail it for HQ." After a moment's thought, I added, "And good luck. It has been an honor fighting by your side."

They nodded, some giving me grim smiles. They were soldiers, and we'd given it the best fight we could. Now, I just wanted to make it to HQ so I could see my parents before they overran us completely. Maybe I'd make it there, I thought as I glanced up into the sky, but—

Oh no. More dragons were streaking down at Ochana from the clouds high above us. Dozens of them, no, *hundreds*, each carrying two riders, some with three. They came at us fast, like falcons diving for prey. "Incoming dragons! Get ready!" I shouted, pointing up at the sky.

Well, we'd done our best, I supposed. There were worse ways to die.

Don't be so dramatic. Did you miss me?

It was Eva's voice in my head! I threw the last bit of my mahier at the diving dragons, extending my senses out to them. Elves, Trolls, even Mermaids, all riding on dragons! And among them flew a swarm of Fairies.

Eva, Cairo, Jericho, and the others had come back with help, at last.

Chapter Twenty-Three

As new dragons and our allies came streaking down, the thick line of Dark Elves, Carnites, and mind-controlled dragons was slowly marching toward Ochana's defenders around the castle and HQ. I had helped rally our troops together to rebuild a defensive line there, but that line looked so thin compared to Eldrick's. The coward hadn't even bothered to come lead his troops himself, he was so confident he'd win. So far, it looked like he had a point.

But then a warning cry went up from his battle line, many of them turning to look up into the sky and point. I even heard a couple panicked screams. Eldrick's battle lines first shuddered, then came to a sloppy halt, though their mind-controlled dragons kept right on going toward the castle defenders. Whatever the crazy dragons were up against, they just kept advancing thanks to Eldrick's mind control.

Our fresh reinforcements plowed into Eldrick's battle line from behind. I saw flashes of light as tilium and mahier flew back and forth. People screamed. In moments, it was hard to tell where Eldrick's line ended and our new troops began. My heart soared with hope! The dragons around the castle could probably handle the mind-controlled dragons still coming at them, without the Dark Elves and Carnites with them.

Then I realized that Eva and our allies, even all fighting together, were still greatly outnumbered. They had the advantages of surprise and hitting the enemy from behind, so it wasn't necessarily hopeless for them.

I was still cut off from the castle, though. "Come on," I shouted to my two squads, "we can't get to the castle, yet, but we can go help our friends out there. They came for us, now let's go help them!"

My soldiers must have been as excited to see reinforcements as I was because for once, they shouted back and raised their swords and spears in the air.

I could see the enemy line getting pushed back, and the buzzing horde of flying enemy dragons in what looked like airplane dogfights with the dragons who came back with Eva, but it wouldn't be long before the bad guys got their act together and hit back. There were just too many of them. I wanted to attack them from the side, or flank them as Jericho called it, when they started pushing back. I shouted for my soldiers to follow me, and we ran up the huge plaza's edge.

Two dragons with wings stretched wide flew toward us from up ahead, coming in low and fast. I couldn't be sure what side they were on, but when I led my squads down a side street, the fliers changed directions.

Enemies, then. "If you have mahier, still, get ready for shields," I said. A few of our people were already out of mahier, and they stepped behind those who still had some. I started pulling mereum together to hit the oncoming enemy with a big downdraft when they got low enough.

Then ten more dragons joined the two coming in, and I felt my heart sinking. Twelve dragons. Once they got closer, I saw that each had two riders, dressed all in black--Dark Elves. We had only seconds left.

When they were fifty feet above the cobblestone roadway, I threw every bit of mereum I had into making hurricane-force winds slam down on them from above. I wanted to plow them right into the pavement! I felt my heart race as the mereum flowed through me, and I could see a faint glow around everything—my eyes radiating mereum-blue due to the amount of energy coursing through me. It was a total rush.

Until nothing happened. The winds were there, I could sense them, but the dragons didn't dip, much less crash. I felt a familiar tingling at the back of my neck. Dark tilium was shielding them. I stared at them in disbelief. It couldn't be him. Why now? Why here?

Before I could think it through, the wing of dragons flew into us. I had to dive to the ground to avoid getting slashed by the claws of dragons flying by at two hundred miles per hour. Their riders leaped off as the dragons hit my squads, using their tilium to land safely, some in front and others behind us. They crouched to one knee to absorb the landing shock. I had hoped they'd hit the ground and go splat, but no such luck.

I dodged to one side as a Dark Elf slashed his sword at me. My counter attack broke his sword near the hilt, just before one of my dragons swung his sword across the Dark Elf's belly and then spun away like a deadly top, still swinging his sword around.

More and more Dark Elves landed among us, and then the dragons started to turn around for another pass.

I felt that tingle again, suddenly, just before a deep rumble came from nowhere and everywhere at once. I could feel it through the ground under my feet. The daylight faded a bit as if a cloud blocked the sun. I glanced up... and paused. The white, pretty clouds of Ochana had become suddenly dark and menacing. More clouds gathered, moving on fast-forward and growing thicker and thicker as they came together over Ochana.

I started to see a red haze around the very edges of the clouds, where daylight would have hit them. The Mediterranean! They looked just like the clouds that hit us when we were flying to Greece from the Congo. I hurled the thought at Eva, though I didn't know where she was, and just hoped she could hear it. "The storm is evil, get down!"

Something was coming through the clouds, something huge. The massive black clouds seemed to expand from inside—a huge face was coming out from within the storm bank. No, it was made of the storm clouds themselves. The mouth opened wide, and I froze in sudden fear as I remembered my dream, the one where Eldrick's giant face chomped on me and I was stuck inside his mouth.

When the mouth opened into a wide grin at the same time thunder boomed with a sound so deep that I felt it in my bones. Vast forks of red lightning shot from Eldrick's cloud-mouth and slammed into the plaza all along the battle lines in the fight between Eldrick's troops and our allies. Wherever the bolts hit, bodies went flying, dragon and Carnite, Elf and Dark Elf. More of Eldrick's troops flew across the battlefield aflame, but he had the troops to spare and we didn't.

I dove for cover, and just in time. Bolts crashed into the ground where I'd been standing. My squads, and the Dark Elves and dragons they had been fighting, scattered in every direction as lightning and thunder pounded both the main battle and its miniature copy where my squads fought his dragon riders.

The lightning stopped, its last rolls of thunder echoing across the plaza. I was half blinded by the lightning's after-images burned into my eyes, but though the lightning had stopped, the face kept coming. Cloud-Eldrick's mouth grew wider and wider, and as I stared down its throat, just before the face smashed into Ochana, I saw a lone figure coming from the cloud-throat, riding on a huge black cloud-dragon. The figure wore a crown and carried a long staff in his hands. I knew that had to be Eldrick, finally coming to his own battle, and he was flying straight at me.

My mind wouldn't accept what I was seeing. I muttered, "No," over and over, and backed away.

Eldrick's voice boomed in my head, loud enough to drop me to my knees with pain. "Keeper. I'm coming to end you," he said simply.

I drew mereum faster than I ever had before, pulling it from the clouds themselves, and hurled it at the cloud-dragon rider. My attack broke apart over him harmlessly, only making the wings seem to flap a little before I was drained. He was almost on me.

I turned and ran. The thing followed, coming on faster and faster. I cut to my left, running between two houses, hoping to lose him in Ochana's maze of homes and alleys.

As it turned out, that was a big mistake. When I came out the other side from between two houses, I found myself in a big courtyard with a high wall along the outside edges, surrounding it on three sides. The only way out was to fly or to go back the way I came, and I wasn't about to fly up with Eldrick's evil magic clouds throwing lightning everywhere and a swarm of crazy dragons attacking everything that moved, so I turned to run back the way I'd come.

I skidded to a halt after only one step. The cloud dragon, almost on top of me, shifted its wings back like an airplane landing, then it burst into a thousand black, snake-like tendrils that collapsed in on themselves in the center until it vanished with a loud pop and only Eldrick remained. His staff, I saw now that he was close enough, was really a huge mace. It looked big enough for a Carnite, I thought, although maybe that was my panic talking.

With his eyes flaring black as if they were made of a shadow-light, he walked toward me and laughed. "Prince Cole, the mighty Keeper of Dragons. Ha! Fight me, Cole. It's time to die."

I sprinted to one side, hoping to get around him and out of the courtyard trap I was in, but he was faster than me even using my tilium to move like a blur.

"Not good enough, dragon." He raised his mace over his head with only one hand, and my eyes bulged in surprise. I couldn't have picked that thing up with two hands, I was pretty sure.

I looked around, frantically, hoping to see friendly soldiers, but there were none there. I was alone with Eldrick in a courtyard, and no one knew it but us.

Eldrick brought his mace down at my head, a wicked grin painted on his face.

I leaped out of the way at the last instant, somersaulted back to my feet, and ran. He struggled to stop his heavy mace, and I ran past him. Freedom!

He pointed two fingers at me and flicked them to one side. I was yanked back like a stuntman in a movie, tied to a train. I flew across the courtyard, landing in a heap in the middle.

Dazed, I scrambled to my feet and drew mereum from the clouds, again, restoring my pool of energy. There was so much mereum that it threatened to overwhelm me in only moments. I snarled and ran at Eldrick. If I couldn't escape, I would have to fight, but I had a trick up my sleeve. As I drew close, he swung his mace again. I used my mahier to deflect it to one side, and it buried itself into the cobblestones.

I poured pure tilium and every bit of my mereum into my sword. My magic sword! The Mere Blade flared cobalt-blue, blindingly bright. It shone bright enough to turn his shadow-glowing eyes blue, even. And by swinging his mace, there was no way he could block my sword.

My heart soared as I leaped through the air, spinning. I passed him on my right and slashed straight out with all my might as I went by. I kept spinning and brought the blade down across his back, diagonally. Two fatal wounds! I landed in a crouch, one knee touching down on the pavement, my arms held out for balance. I felt the explosion of mereum and tilium flare out from Eldrick like a concussion behind me. I calmly stood and turned, grinning.

And froze. My attack had almost cut his shirt off of him, but where my first strike landed, there was only a faint trickle of blood. As I watched, the thin wound closed up completely. I was staring where he should have been nearly cut in half when a mountain smashed into my right side. That's what it felt like, at least, when his giant mace smacked me. I streaked through the air and smashed into the courtyard's stone wall faster than I could begin to throw up any kind of shield. The wall cracked from the force of my impact, and I bounced off. When I landed on my back on the cobblestones, I couldn't get up, no matter how hard I tried. I could move my arms a little bit, but not enough to swing a weapon. Anyway, I didn't have my sword anymore. I didn't know where it went, but I couldn't have reached it even if I knew.

Eldrick strolled up to me, the mace over his shoulder, and my eyes went wide. He smirked at me, the heavy-weight prizefighter looking down at some chump kid who never had a chance.

"Nicely done, Cole. If you had another one of those attacks in you, it's possible you could actually hurt me. You drained most of my tilium with that attack. But it was too little, too late, kiddo. Unlike Doctor Evil, I don't think a quick, painless death is too good for my enemies. I'd love to stay and chat, reveal my big plan, and give you a chance to escape, but instead, I think I'll just kill you. Tell Jago I said hello when you see your Ancestors."

"I'd rather... you... tell him." It was hard to get the words out. So much for my witty last words.

He snorted, still smirking, but didn't waste any more time. He raised his mace up with both hands and it cast a shadow as big as me. I couldn't rip my eyes off it as he began his deadly swing.

Chapter Twenty-Four

Time slowed down almost to a stop. I noticed the strangest things, like the way the sunlight shone off the black clouds in a red hue that almost looked like they were on fire from inside. Or the thick gash in Eldrick's mace, and how dirt drifted away from it from when he'd smashed it into the plaza's cobblestone floor. I noticed his eyes were wide with excitement, thrilled at the idea of smashing my head into that same floor.

I threw my arm up to protect myself, purely by reflex since there was no way that would save me, but then my eyes were drawn to my hand. The ring Prince Jago gave me was on my index finger, now risen to the surface and pulsing with a pure, cobalt glow. Hadn't it become invisible when I put it on? Hadn't it merged into my skin? Not anymore, though. Now it was brightly shining, gleaming in the sunlight.

Eldrick swung his huge mace down at me with his face twisted into a furious snarl, lips curled back to bare his teeth, mouth open in a roar I couldn't hear in the silence of that slow-motion moment. I looked away from him and back at the ring. I wanted the last thing I ever saw to be something beautiful, not him and his ugly face. From the corner of my eye, I saw his mace looming over me, blocking out the sun like it was about to block out my life.

The ring pulsed brighter, twice. There was a huge flare that made me close my eyes, but it stayed painfully, blindingly bright even through my closed eyelids. The light felt cool and comfortable on my skin, though, like it knew me and was brushing its hand over my arm tenderly.

I heard a scream. I opened my eyes as the flare faded away and saw Eldrick flying backward across the plaza. He landed hard, on his back, and the air between us shimmered like heat rising off a long, empty road on a hot day. I almost thought I saw figures in the shimmer. I blinked.

When I opened my eyes, I was *sure* of it; people started as just outlines, then filled in from the edges inward. There were four of them, all shades of white even when they finished becoming visible, like someone had taken a cell phone picture with a photo-negative filter.

One looked over his shoulder at me, and I jumped halfway out of my own skin in surprise when I realized who he was. Jago! The Ancestors! The ones who had given me the ring, which I'd forgotten all about. They had said it would make itself known when the time was right.

The four Ancestors sprinted toward Eldrick as he climbed to his feet. The way their robes and clothes and long hair blew back, they looked like they were running into a heavy wind, but to me, the air was perfectly still. Their weapons, the same white-cartoon color as the Ancestors themselves, flashed in the sunlight as the four struck Eldrick at the same time.

The force knocked him back down to his knees and I thought I saw him flicker. They hit him with their swords again and again, and each time, he flickered more and seemed to grow weaker until I could almost see through him.

But I didn't see any blood.

Then he burst into motion, leaping to his feet and sending the four Ancestors flying back in every direction. He jumped through the air at Jago, who had landed on his back, and smashed his mace down. It passed through the Ancestor harmlessly, though, cracking the plaza floor. He struck again, but it went through Jago just like the first time.

Then another Ancestor struck Eldrick from behind. Eldrick flickered and staggered, going down to one knee. The Ancestors surrounded him again and continued striking him with their swords, moving in a blur of speed.

I scrambled to my feet while I stared. I didn't know what to do. They were doing more than I could, already. With every sword blow, Eldrick looked less and less solid, but he didn't fade away to nothing, even after a dozen more blows.

Jago shouted into my head, "We can't kill him! Feel his dark tilium—it's sustaining him. We can fight him off, but the dead have no power over tilium. Run, Nephew."

Tilium was keeping him alive? I opened my dragon senses and reached out, looking at Eldrick. They were right—he had so much tilium in him that it was leaking out where the Ancestors' swords hit. It was like blood that I could only see with my dragon-sight, but there was so much tilium inside him that he'd never bleed it all out.

I felt a tingling in the middle of my chest, from my heart. The tingle spread from there, growing down my arms, down my body. I'd felt this before, I realized, in the jungles of South America with the Farro.

As the tingles reached my ankles and wrists, I felt myself rise up into the air like a marionette on strings, arms and legs dangling behind me. Glowing silver tendrils, like a thick mass of spider webs, shot out of my fingers and toes.

The tingle flowed up through my neck, too. I threw my head back, and the silver threads burst out of my mouth and even my eyes. The tendrils had a mind of their own. They did what they wanted. I could feel their urgent need as they raced to Eldrick. I heard him scream, and he sounded afraid.

Good. That thought strengthened me, and when I stopped struggling against them, even more threads came out of my mouth, my hands, my feet. They struck him and wrapped around him, a fly in a spider's silk cocoon. He thrashed wildly, but my energy was too strong for him to resist.

Then the threads drew tight. They pulled back into me slowly, at the same time dragging Eldrick toward me just like the Farro had when I took their dark tilium. I was going to devour Eldrick. I was going to be stronger than anyone had ever been, with all that tilium inside me. All the tilium in the world, it felt like. It was all mine, and all I had to do was take it from Eldrick.

Jago's voice inside my head said, "Colton. You must stop. If you draw him in, he'll poison your soul. Stop!"

I couldn't, though. I wasn't in control of the threads now any more than I had been when this happened before. "I don't know how!" I screamed.

Eldrick was halfway across the plaza. In seconds, he'd be with me. I didn't know what to expect, but I knew it was going to be bad for me.

I focused everything I could, all my willpower. "Stop!"

The threads kept pulling him toward me, ignoring my command. He was only feet away from me, thrashing and struggling with fear-filled eyes, trying to get away from me.

The ring...

I had an idea. I sent my mahier out to Eldrick and it wrapped around him like a second skin. Then I sent my purified tilium at him. It wrapped around him in cords thick as cables, binding him tightly. And lastly, I pulled mereum from the water vapor in the air, the humidity, even my own sweat. The mereum blob's edges moved outward over him, *tick, tick tick*, each bit stretching out over him like a potter moving clay with his thumbs. Finally, it surrounded him completely.

That was when the tendrils and my mereum fought each other. One tried to pull Eldrick into me, and the other I willed to pull him into the ring instead of me. It took so much effort, two drops of sweat fell off my chin. I couldn't keep that up, I realized.

But as panic threatened to overcome me, I felt a hand on my shoulder. Somehow, I knew Jago stood beside me. I grew calmer. I could do it. The Ancestors had faith in me.

Slowly at first, but then faster and faster, the tendrils lost their grip. They turned thin and frail, and one after the other, they snapped in half. The broken tilium ends slithered back into my body, leaving only the mereum. I knew what I had to do, then.

I tried again to will my mereum to pull Eldrick's power into the ring. He had so much of it! But the ring, I knew somehow, was strong enough to hold even Eldrick. Eldrick began to stretch out like silly putty. The instant part of that stretched-out soul touched the ring, it began sucking him in. First, it pulled what looked like his actual shadow out of him. It stretched thin as it was sucked into the ring.

I realized that, without his tainted tilium, there would be no Eldrick left. His power had long ago overwhelmed him, destroying every other part of himself until only that evil remained. He was made of the dark tilium I was forcing into the ring.

At the end, there was a whooshing noise that started low and deep, but then rose higher and higher until it was shrill and piercing, like the winds of a tornado blowing all around us. All of a sudden, the shrill train-whistle noise was cut off in one abrupt moment.

The air grew still. The black angry clouds above paused, paled slowly to white, and then faded away entirely.

I staggered and fell to my knees. I didn't have to look around to know the Ancestors were gone, just as Eldrick was. They left when he had. I silently thanked them for saving me until I discovered how to defeat our enemy.

As my strength returned, I climbed back to my feet. I looked for the Mere Blade and found it lying in a corner. I held out my hand toward it. It rattled, then flew through the air to me. I caught it in one hand and felt the ring grow warmer.

I had wanted the blade and it came to me. I could feel the almost unlimited power I possessed. The dark tilium called to me. It told me to do things. I could end everything if I wanted. All of it. Dragons,

Dark Elves, darkness. I could destroy it all and go home to my human parents.

I shook my head. Those weren't my thoughts. The ring's stored power was calling me to use it. Fine, I decided, I would use it—just not the way the corrupted tilium wanted me to.

I raised my hands out to my sides, palms up, until they were at shoulder height. Then I turned my hands over and swung them toward the ground. "Down!" I shouted. Above, the swarm of thrashing, fighting dragons stopped in mid-air, then streaked toward the ground as though yanked down, hard.

"Stay!" I yelled. The rain of dragons stopped just before hitting the ground and then stayed there, immobile.

I had the power to end the war. At last, I could save the world, and I'd use Eldrick's own power to do it. I loved the irony. I stormed out of the plaza, heading toward the fighting.

A block away, I saw maybe two dozen Dark Elves and a Carnite fighting half a dozen Woland warriors. I flicked my hand to one side, and the Dark Elves and the Carnite flew up, away, and over the edge of Ochana, screaming the whole way.

The dragons turned to look at me, confused. I ignored them and kept walking. Every time I saw a crazed dragon, I could almost see the knot of dark tilium in its head, binding its thoughts. It was child's play to flick those away, and when they were gone, the dragons were free. Confused about where they were, but free.

I saved all the crazed dragons I could. I killed whatever Dark Elves and Carnites I saw. None had a chance against me, not with the power I had in the palm of my hand. It didn't take long for the fighting to stop, because there was no one left to fight. My dragons were safe, while Eldrick's army went on the run or died.

The battle was over. The world and Ochana were safe once more. But all I wanted was to find Eva, Cairo, Jericho, and all my other friends. I had to make sure they were safe.

After pausing and debating it, I pulled the ring off my finger and put it in my pocket where it couldn't cause any mischief.

The Crowns' Accord

Chapter Twenty-Five

The Congo was beautiful as we walked through the little pathway the Elves had grown, stretching from Paraiso to the clearing. The shoulder strap on my kilt dug into my neck, and the sweat from jungle heat didn't help.

Eva swatted my hand aside. "Knock it off. You'll wrinkle it."

"I never wore one before," I said.

Ochana's formalwear was a ceremonial kilt, like the ones Highlander Regiments wore in Scotland. Which kind of dragon one was made for determined the dominant color, except for the silver dragons. Theirs were all black fabric with lots of silver highlights and lines. I actually thought theirs looked way better than mine.

"Well," Eva said, "I think you can deal with it long enough to sit through Gaber's coronation. It's not every day the Elves get a new king, and it's kind of surprising we were invited."

We arrived at the clearing just then. It was the same clearing I'd spoken to the Ancestors in when they'd given me the ring. I was surprised the coronation wasn't being held at the lake in Paraiso, the source of their tilium, but then I saw the huge crowd and the choice made more sense. There wouldn't have been enough room for everyone by the lake.

"Look, there are your parents," Eva said, bouncing on the balls of her feet and pointing. "They're with Queen Annabelle of the Fairies and Queen Delsa of the Mermaids."

I said, "King Evander and Princess Clara, too. Did you ever think you'd see all of them sitting together and actually laughing?"

Cairo, standing on Eva's other side, chuckled. "Never did think it would happen. This is the first time I've ever seen it. I hear Gaber has a special announcement to make during his coronation, too."

He winked at me, because I was in on it, too. We all knew he was going to announce the Crowns'

Accord. King Rylan, as king of the dragons, would normally have that honor but times had changed. Dragons changed it when we turned our backs on the world. Gaber announcing the new accord would go a long way toward healing those old wounds.

Jericho's voice, right behind me, made me jump with surprise as he said, "Rylan is more generous than I'd be."

Eva and Cairo grinned at me when I jumped. Embarrassed at being startled, I snapped, "That's why he's the king and you're the warrior."

"Truth." He put his hand on my shoulder and joined our little circle, ignoring my outburst.

Zane stepped up on my other side. He didn't say anything, but nodded to everyone, greeting us. Then we made our way to our seats, Zane sitting with us instead of with his brother. I wasn't sure what that was about, but I didn't complain. After the battle, he and I had become a lot closer.

All around us, the clothes were impressive. Everyone had on their very finest outfits, most of it newly-made and all very formal. It still made me uncomfortable. I was used to jeans and sweats.

Worse, the coronation itself wouldn't happen for another hour, and I fidgeted the entire time. First, the kings and queens made their speeches praising Gaber, swearing to protect each other always. I guessed that was to set the stage for announcing the Crowns' Accord later.

After the boring speeches, the coronation was done. As amazing as the ceremony was, it only took a few minutes, which was disappointing. And then Gaber's speech afterward, while wearing the ancient Elven crown and looking rather impressive, took another twenty minutes. I thought he did a great job. It had to be kind of scary standing in front of so many people, even kings and queens, and trying to remember the speech he wanted to make. He did well, though, and there was a lot of applause when he finished.

After that, Gaber left the stage and went to his throne, and then came the part I didn't want to sit through. Everyone with any authority at all got the chance to make a speech and be seen with the new king, and none of them passed up the chance.

Cairo said, "Poor Gaber. We aren't going to sit through this whole thing, are we? They're going to open the buffet soon. A dragon's gotta eat, you know."

"Actually," I said, "I have something I want to talk to you all about. I need your help, though. Will you come with me?" I looked at my friends, but I also included Zane. Jericho was gone, since he also had to make a speech, and had disappeared after the crowning.

When they all nodded, I said, "Okay, follow me."

We made our way through the crowd, trying not to bump into men in tuxedos or step on the beautiful dresses. Finally, we got through them and were able to go deeper into the jungle, away from the clearing. As we walked, amazingly, my kilt made it easy to climb over big roots, logs, and so on. And it had pockets! Our little walk in the jungle gave me a new appreciation for kilts.

We reached a smaller clearing in the Congo jungle. In the center was a tree stump. Some human must have recently cut it down with a chainsaw, because the cut was flat and smooth, and the wood hadn't yet aged gray. It was perfect for what I had in mind.

I pulled out the ring the Ancestors had given me, the one with Eldrick's evil soul trapped inside. Just looking at it made me want to put it on. The ring, it called to me. I had to count to ten with my eyes closed to keep myself from doing it. And that was the reason I'd brought them all out to the middle of the jungle.

"Eva, you're my best friend. Cairo, you've become a friend, even though I didn't like you at first." I paused, grinning, and they chuckled politely. I continued, "And Zane, you proved yourself during Eldrick's attack on Ochana. I doubted you right up until then. I'd like to get to know you better, now that this is all over with, and to be friends with my father's brother."

Zane nodded, half-smiling back at me. He was always hard to read.

Eva said, "What's with the ring? Did you learn something else it does? Hurry up and show us!"

"Actually, I did learn something else. The thing is evil now that Eldrick is in it. I feel my blood drawn to it, if that makes any sense."

"Not really." Eva smirked at me.

"I feel a constant urge to put it on, and then to do bad things with it. You have no idea how much power the ring has—how much power it gives me."

Cairo said, "I kind of do know how much power it has. I was there. I saw how you marched through the battlefield smiting Dark Elves and Carnites like a god. It was amazing. No enemy could ever stand up to Ochana again, not with that ring on our side."

I shook my head, my lips pressed tightly together. I set the ring on the tree stump and said, "That's the point. I felt like a god. I don't think anyone should have so much power. It's too tempting. And Eldrick's spirit is in there, calling me."

Zane said, "What are you trying to say?"

I took a deep breath. "I think we should destroy it. We're safer destroying it than using it."

Cairo's jaw dropped. "You can't be serious. With that ring, Ochana is unbeatable."

Eva was opening and closing her fists, shifting from one foot to the other. She said, "I agree with Cole. What if someone put it on and the ring overpowered them? Cole's saying it's hard to resist the urges it gives him, and if he has a hard time, out of everyone I know, then we should get rid of it. Anyway, it gives me an eerie feeling. I don't like it."

Zane stepped up to the stump and looked down at the ring. Everyone turned to see what he'd do. Would he go for the ring? I had a barrier of mereum ready to go, just in case.

"Cole is right," he said, his gaze still locked onto the ring. "I felt it calling to me as soon as Cole said we should destroy it. It wants me to put it on. I could be the king, it says. I don't want to be the king, but it makes me want it. Or it brings out something in my subconscious."

"Either way, that's bad," Eva muttered.

"Either way. And one more thing is that you can't watch it twenty-four-seven. What if someone stole it? I could steal it right now, you know..."

As his voice trailed off, I knew I was right and the ring had to go. I looked at Cairo and tilted my head toward Zane; Cairo stepped up and got between Zane and the ring, pushing him back gently.

Zane's cheeks got red and he grinned sheepishly. "See what I mean?"

Yes, I did. I got everyone to stand in a circle around the stump. Once I made the decision for real, I suddenly just wanted to get it over with. Before I could talk myself out of it.

"Well, let's get this over with. Summon your dragons," I said, and transitioned almost instantly into mine, with its multi-colored scales.

Eva was just as unusual, her golden scales gleaming in the light of the sun that streamed down through the gap in the trees overhead. Cairo looked plain beside her, as did Zane.

One. Two. Three!

The four of us poured our dragonfire onto the ring. At first, the flames didn't do anything to the ring, though the stump disintegrated in seconds under so much dragonfire. We kept the fire going, though. I counted the time in my head. Six... Seven...

At eight, whatever was protecting it gave out. The ring suddenly melted into a pool, and then even that burned away in our magic dragonfire. Only when it was gone did we stop flaming it, and shifted back into our humans.

Eva was, as usual, the first to say something. "Did you feel it? Like, when the ring disintegrated, I felt the sun get brighter, the grass greener, the air was better."

Zane said, "I thought it was just me. Yes, I felt it. I think that's when Eldrick was finally destroyed forever."

Cairo snorted, grinning. "Good riddance."

Yep, good riddance, indeed. It was truly over only once Eldrick's spirit was gone. Until that moment, it hadn't truly felt like the war was over, even though we'd beaten all his armies and sent them packing, sucked him into a magic ring, and healed all the blackness over the Earth.

"So." I scratched my neck where the kilt was again itchy, back in my human form.

Cairo shrugged. "So. Can we go hit the buffet now?"

Eva punched him in the arm, grinning, and then we all made our way back to the coronation, and the buffet of course. Soon, we'd be heading back to Ochana. The thought made my heart beat faster, and I walked a little faster, too. Home. Paraiso would always be like a second home to me, but Ochana was where I belonged, and after the war we had all just been through, there was a lot of work to be done there. Ochana needed its prince now more than ever.

"We'll leave right after the coronation stuff ends, yeah?" I asked the others.

Eva nodded, sliding her arm around Cairo's waist, and Zane pursed his lips, nodding, too. They looked at peace, finally, like they'd found their place in the world.

A world that was finally also at peace.

Books by J.A. Culican

Novels

The Prince Returns-Keeper of Dragons book 1

The Elven Alliance-Keeper of Dragons book 2

The Mere Treaty-Keeper of Dragons book 3

The Crowns' Accord-Keeper of Dragons book 4

Second Sight-Hollows Ground book 1

Slayer-Dragon Tamer book 1

Warrior-Dragon Tamer book 2

Protector-Dragon Tamer book 3

Short Stories

The Golden Dragon-Keeper of Dragons short story

Jericho-Keeper of Dragons short story

Phoenix-Hollows Ground short story

Savior-Dragon Tamer short story

About the author

About J.A. Culican

J.A. Culican is a USA Today Bestselling author of the middle grade fantasy series Keeper of Dragons. Her first novel in the fictional series catapulted a trajectory of titles and awards, including top selling author on the USA Today bestsellers list and Amazon, and a rightfully earned spot as an international best seller. Additional accolades include Best Fantasy Book of 2016, Runner-up in Reality Bites Book Awards, and 1st place for Best Coming of Age Book from the Indie book Awards.

J.A. Culican holds a Master's degree in Special Education from Niagara University, in which she has been teaching special education for over 12 years. She is also the president of the autism awareness non-profit Puzzle Peace United. J.A. Culican resides in Southern New Jersey with her husband and four young children.

Contact me

I can't wait to hear from you!

Email:
jaculican@gmail.com

Website:
http://jaculican.com

Facebook Author Page:
https://www.facebook.com/jaculican

Amazon Author Page:
http://amazon.com/author/jaculican

Twitter:
https://twitter.com/jaculican

Instagram:
http://instagram.com/jaculican

Pinterest:
http://pinterest.com/jaculican

Add me on Goodreads here:
https://www.goodreads.com/author/show/15287808.J_A_Culican